No Boyz
Allowed

Also by Ni-Ni Simone

SHORTIE LIKE MINE

IF I WAS YOUR GIRL

A GIRL LIKE ME

TEENAGE LOVE AFFAIR

UPGRADE U

THE BREAK-UP DIARIES, VOL. 1

HOLLYWOOD HIGH (with Amir Abrams)

Published by Kensington Publishing Corporation

No Boyz Allowed

NI-NI SIMONE

Dafina KTeen Books
KENSINGTON PUBLISHING CORP.
http://www.kensingtonbooks.com

DAFINA KTEEN BOOKS are published by

Kensington Publishing Corp.
119 West 40th Street
New York, NY 10018

All Kensington titles, imprints, and distributed lines are available at special quantity discounts for bulk purchases for sales promotion, premiums, fund-raising, educational, or institutional use.

Special book excerpts or customized printings can also be created to fit specific needs. For details, write or phone the office of the Kensington Special Sales Manager: Attn.: Special Sales Department. Kensington Publishing Corp., 119 West 40th Street, New York, NY 10018. Phone: 1-800-221-2647.

KTeen Reg. US Pat. & TM Off.
Sunburst logo Reg. US Pat. & TM Off.

ISBN-13: 978-0-7582-4193-1
ISBN-10: 0-7582-4193-3

First Printing: August 2012
10 9 8 7 6 5 4 3 2 1

Printed in the United States of America

To the Gems of the world—
know that as long as there is God,
there is Love.
And wherever there is love,
there is always hope.
And wherever there is hope,
there is always the ability to
be anything you want to be!

Brown beauty
is limitless.
It is not confined to the size of your thighs
the color of your eyes
or your bra size...
It has nothing to do with your waist,
your face,
or how nice that cutie told you your booty was...
It is not bound by religion
race
creed
your mama,
her mama
big mama's mama...
It is immeasurable
unstoppable
fierce
fly
and oh so fabulous...
It cannot be bound by circumstance
happenstance
or a missed chance...
It does not die
it does not fly
it dreams
and loves
and believes
that it can be anything
it wants to be...
It is a quiet rebel
a lady with a cause
a little girl with a mission
standing tall
and demanding for the world to see
that she
is Brown beauty!

ACKNOWLEDGMENTS

All thanks to my Father, God, and His Son, Jesus, for loving me and blessing me. My prayer is that I am able to take the blessings You have bestowed upon me and be a blessing to someone else.

To my parents for always being my champions.

To my husband and my children for making me laugh and for being the best family anyone can have!

To my daughter, Taylor, for the quick morning reads.

To my little cousin and assistant, Korynn, for always being there one chapter at a time!

To my family, thanks for your support!

To Keisha Ervin for being seventeen with me no matter how old we really are!

To all of my friends, thank you for your love and encouragement!

To my brother from another mother, Amir Abrams. How sweet is it that the Universe aligned our steps so that we could take that train ride from Manhattan to Newark, become spiritual siblings, and have our destinies unfold before us. And to think the best is yet to come! So, in short, I'll simply say that I'll see you for high tea at the estate!

To my editor, Selena James. Thank you for your patience, your talent, and most of all, for the push and belief you have in me!

To my Kensington-Dafina-KTeen family, thank you for

everything! As I often say, I may have written the manuscript, but together we made this a book.

To my agent Sara Camilli, you are truly the best!

To the bookstores, the blogs, sales teams, the librarians, the students, the schools, and the parents who have introduced my work to their teens, I thank you for bringing me into your lives, your homes, and your stores. I appreciate all of the support, the e-mails, and the letters. Thank you for letting me know that my work truly makes a difference.

Saving the best for last, the fans! I can't thank you enough for the joy you bring me. I thank you for your support and encouragement. Here's to an unlimited amount of best sellers! Be sure to keep the e-mails coming: ninisimone @yahoo.com. Also visit my Website: www.ninisimone.com.

One love,
Ni-Ni Simone

1

Brick City, USA

The moment the soles of my crisp white Concords hit
the concrete and my brother and I stood in front of
our new foster home—our third one this year, our
umpteenth this lifetime—I knew this was destined to be a
hot mess.

Some ish, fa'real.

And there was no way we were staying here.

Straight up.

Seriously, I'd been in foster homes since I was nine—so
I could tell the strict from the don't-give-a-damn; the
halfway decent from the get-me-the-hell-out-of-here; and
the money whores from the fake saviors. So, based on
sight alone, I knew these fools were all of the above.

"Hey, how y'all doing?" Apparently, that was the head of
the foster-home welcoming committee. "I'm Cousin
Shake."

I blinked not once, but twice. *What the heck is a
Cousin Shake and what...in the bejesus...does he have*

on? Sparkling rainbow doo-rag, rainbow sequin short-set, and black gazelle glasses with no lenses. And wait, hold up...Hold. Up. Is he rockin' high-top L.A. Gears on his feet?

What the...

Cousin Shake continued, "And this is my boo." He pointed to a five-foot-tall honey-colored woman standing next to him.

"I'm Ms. Minnie," she said. "Welcome, sweets!"

I couldn't believe this. Not only did Ms. Minnie have on the same exact short-set as Cousin Shake, she wore a curly-blond lace-front wig with the hairline practically glued on her eyebrows. Nasty. And to make matters worse, she smiled at me and on the right side of her mouth were two gold teeth: one on the top and the other on the bottom. Gross.

Know what? Maybe I'm crazy and none of this is real. I clicked the heels of my sneakers together. Nothing. I was still in Oz a.k.a. Newark, New Jersey. Better known as hell.

"Hi, Cousin Shake," my eight-year-old brother Malik said, grinning.

I sucked my teeth. Clearly Malik didn't listen. He knew he was supposed to follow my lead and speak when I said to speak, but instead he gave Cousin Shake a high-five like they were boys. "Wassup?"

"You got it, baby." Cousin Shake clicked his tongue. "Know what, baby, you a lil chunky like me." He continued, proudly, "So maybe I'll change the baby up and call you Baby-Tot-Tot, you know, short for toddler."

"Word." Malik nodded and smiled in amazement. "Yeah, I like that. Baby-Tot-Tot. That's hot."

Oh heck no! "Malik, get yo behind over here," I snapped.

And yeah, everybody's heads turned and they all looked at me like I was crazy, but so what? "You must be trippin'! *Baby Tot-Tot,* did you have crack in your cereal this morning?"

"We didn't eat this morning." Malik shook his head and looked at me confused. "You know that foster mother had our things packed and us standing on the curb for two days. She told me don't even think about eating!"

I placed my hands on my hips. "It wasn't two days it was just today and you get my point." I turned to Cousin Shake and said, "Get this straight, my brother's name is Malik and if you can't call him that, don't call him at all!" I spun on my heels toward Ms. Thomas, my caseworker. The look on her face said that she was ready to dump us and get back to her office. But the look on my face let her know that wouldn't be happening anytime soon. "Get us out of here!"

Ms. Thomas's eyes pleaded with me. "Give them a chance. Please behave. They're nice people."

"Oh no, oh no, oh no—" Cousin Shake stuttered. "We don't beg children to behave, we chop 'em in the throat and make 'em do it!"

Chop 'em in the throat? I wish somebody would... Hmph, this old dude really don't know me. I snapped my fingers and swung my neck—practically into a 360. "You might wanna bring that down, Cousin Crazy."

"What kinda boom-boom-bull is this? Hold me back, Minnie!" Cousin Shake spat as he spun around, broke out into the cat daddy, and topped it off with the bounce. "Hold me back!"

Am I dreaming? Am. I. Dreaming? Why is he dancing?

I looked at my caseworker and she looked at her watch.

"Let it slide, Shake," Ms. Minnie said, stretching out her arms before Cousin Shake. "Let it slide. She ain't ready for you, Shakadean. She. Ain't. Ready. For. You."

"Hell nawl, she ain't ready, 'cause I will slide some bilingual on dat. Cousin Shake-O ain't the one-O. Comprend-O? So, what you ain't 'bout to do-O—"

"You're here!" An excited voice interrupted Cousin Shake's stupid tirade, and before I could turn to see where the voice had come from, this woman had snatched a hug from me and quickly followed up by hugging and kissing my brother on both cheeks. "I didn't know you were coming so early," the woman said, now shaking my caseworker's hand. "I'm Grier and this is my husband, Khalil." She pointed to a tall and dark brown man who held two large Target bags. "We're the foster parents. Well, we're all a family, us, Cousin Shake, Ms. Minnie, and my children. We live here together." She pointed to the house in front of us.

I quickly scanned the two-story colonial, with the large front and backyard, and the long and wide driveway with the seven-foot basketball hoop at the top of it. For a moment, I wondered if these clowns were hustling. Then I looked back at them, soaked in how ridiculous they were, and knew right away that they were too played to be hustling anything other than a nine-to-five. I was definitely in Squareville.com.

Ms. Grier carried on, "I'm so sorry we're late. But we were picking up some things for the kids' rooms." She beamed in excitement. "I could hardly sleep last night I was so nervous about you all coming. I hope you're hungry, because Ms. Minnie cooked a feast! So let's go inside."

"I thought I smelled a meal!" Malik said, letting my hand go and reaching for Ms. Grier.

"Shut up," I snapped. "You don't smell anything." I snatched his hand back.

"Grier," Cousin Shake tried to whisper but failed. "What kinda lil baby-lifers tryna bring up in here? If you want me and Minnie to leave, all you have to do is tell us."

"I'm not a lifer, thank you!" I wiggled my neck. "I'm Gem!"

"Cousin Shake," Ms. Grier said, agitated. "Would you and Ms. Minnie please cut it out?" She looked back at me and smiled. "Honey, you'll get used to them."

I twisted my lips and popped my eyes. "No I won't, 'cause I don't do old *and* crazy." I turned to my case-worker. "I know you can see that these people are nuts!"

Cousin Shake broke out into his cat daddy and bounce routine again. "Lawd, please take away these evil thoughts running through my mind. Take away the thoughts about how I need to go inside, grab my belt, and whoop dat—"

"Cousin Shake!" Ms. Grier yelled. "Don't cuss at these children."

Cousin Shake snorted. "Okay, then let me put it like this." He looked me dead in my eyes. "Some-bleep-bleepin'-body need to bust yo bleep-bleepin' bleep. 'Cause if you keep tryin' me it's gon' be a mother-suckin' bleep-bleepin' prob-lem." He took a step back and mouthed, "Now try me. Please." He arched a brow. "I bleepin' dare you."

"Gem, you have to be respectful!" Ms. Thomas squealed, embarrassed.

Oh no she didn't! "You don't tell me what to do!"

"Gem." Ms. Thomas spoke in a low and patient tone. "I'm

trying really hard to find you a home, but at sixteen I need you to work with me. Now, I have done my part. I have found you home, after home, after home, but your behavior causes you to be removed from everywhere we place you. I *need you* to help me to help you."

"Whatever." I flipped my hand dismissively.

She continued, "I know you're hurting."

I rolled my eyes. I hated when people tried to analyze me. And besides, I wasn't hurt I was pissed off. "It's not that serious," I assured her. "I'm just ready to leave."

Ms. Grier said, "Try to give us a chance. My mother died when I was a teen and my sister and brothers lived different places until Cousin Shake took us all in and raised us together. So I understand what you're going through, but I think if you gave us a chance you'll like staying here. I have twin daughters, both in college. Toi, the oldest, is here in New Jersey. She has a son, Noah. My youngest daughter, Seven, is away in New Orleans at Stiles U."

For a moment my eyes brightened up. I always wanted to go to Stiles U.

"Maybe I can arrange something where you can visit Seven on campus."

My eyes narrowed. "I'm not interested."

"Well, hopefully that will change." She smiled. "I also have a son, Amir. We call him Man-Man."

"How old is he?" Malik asked, excited.

"Seventeen."

"Seventeen!" Malik gasped. "A big brother!" He turned to me. "Can we at least have some chicken and Kool-Aid before we go?" Malik begged, like he was starving. "I swear it smells like K.F.C."

If looks could kill, Malik would be cremated. I hated

that he was so needy! Always begging somebody! I was embarrassed and the more I stood here, the more I thought about how I needed to leave. To hell with this caseworker and this ridiculous family. I was over it.

I looked at Malik and said, "How about this. If you rolling with me, then let's go. If not, then peace, 'cause I'm out. I'll see you around." I hesitated for a moment and when Malik didn't budge, I felt a swift kick to my gut. I took a few steps backward as I struggled to hide the tears that filled my eyes. "You're really not coming with me?" I said, more to myself than to Malik.

When he didn't answer, I sucked in a breath, hit them all with a two-finger peace sign, and took off down the street; and as I rounded the corner I heard Ms. Grier say, "We have to go after her!"

2

I decided I was doing me.
Period.

And I hated to leave my brother, but with the way I felt, if he wanted to stay in that foster home with Cousin Creepy, then that was on him.

Seriously.

I had things to do.

Places to be.

Which was why I walked into Newark Penn Station with my back arched and my confidence on overload. I needed a fresh start—a new beginning. And for once in my life *I* was going to decide where *I* wanted to go, not where the caseworker wanted to place me. Screw that. I was blowing this place and the nightmare that came with it.

I considered a few cities where I could start over.

Washington, D.C.?

A smile ran across my face.

Boom, there it was. Endless parties, Obama-land, and a chance to have a drama-free start and stamp my independence. Yeah, that was it. D.C.-bound.

I cheesed from ear to ear as I proudly stepped in line and waited my turn to see the ticket agent.

I was determined to do it and do it big. Once I arrived in my newfound promised land, I would figure things out from there.

The closer I got to the front of the line I couldn't help but notice the ticket prices.

Washington, D.C. was sixty-five dollars.

I hope like hell they took I.O.U.'s . . .

"Excuse me," the ticket agent interrupted my thoughts. "May I help you?"

I nervously bit the corner of my lip and leaned from one foot to the next.

Confidence.

"Umm, yes, that's a very good question you just asked me." I did my best to speak with perfect diction. This way she wouldn't think I was crazy. "I was wondering if you would be so graciously kind and wonderful and let me know if you can, umm, give me a ticket to Washington, D.C., and I, umm, could come back next week and pay for it?" I shot her a quick Barbie-doll smile and as my single dimple sank into my right cheek, I batted my long lashes, stood back, and waited for an answer.

"Excuse me?" The agent looked at me as if she was two seconds from calling security. "We don't do that."

"Okay, ummm . . . yeah. I was just checkin'," I said as I maintained the dumbest smile in the world. Then I stepped out of line and sauntered to the back of the station.

Damn.

I sat down on one of the hard wooden benches and tossed my head between my knees. My hair swept from my shoulders forward and for a brief second I wished that I could disappear.

3

Public Service Announcement: I am pissed.org.

How did I fall asleep in Penn Station? How did I let the police catch me? How did I end up in the back of my case-worker's green Chevy Malibu...again? And how did I get hand-delivered back to hell was all beyond me....

Something was definitely wrong with this picture.

"You are a beautiful young woman," Ms. Thomas said, as if she'd just blessed me with a brilliant idea.

Yeah...yeah...yeah...Heard that before. I rolled my eyes toward the roof of the car.

"And unfortunately at the moment your circumstances aren't the greatest."

"Whew." I twirled my left index finger in the air and said sarcastically, "You're really catching on."

"Gem, you have to want more. You have to, because I can't want more for you than you want for yourself—"

"And what do you want for me?!" I snapped. "For me to

be taken off your caseload? Spare me." I flicked my hand dismissively.

"Gem, I know how you feel—"

I chuckled in disbelief. "I'm sooooo sick of that line. Really, I am. 'Cause for-real-for-real, you don't know nothing about me! All you know is that you want my case closed."

"That's not true, Gem. I want what's best for you. I really do and you may not see it now but you need a family."

"I don't need a family!" Unwanted tears filled my eyes and no matter how I tried to hold them back, they ran down my cheeks. "I'm good by myself! I got this!"

"Gem, I just want you to give these people a chance."

"I don't have to give them anything. You pay them room and board for me, that's enough!"

"This family seems to really care, Gem. Do you know that they called me every hour, on the hour, to see if I had heard from you or if you'd returned?"

"And doesn't that sound a little freaky to you? They don't even know me. Why would they be sweatin' me like that?!"

"They care."

"Yeah," I rolled my eyes toward the roof again. "Everybody cares," I held my fingers out as if I were counting on them. "Everybody wants to make a difference, everybody knows how I feel, and everybody's been sixteen. Yada, yada, yada, what-the-heck-ever. Because from where I'm sitting, if everybody's been in my shoes, then why hasn't anybody told me why my mother is a crackhead? And who's my daddy? Huh? Answer me that? How come I've been in three high schools and I'm only a sophomore?" I paused. "You know why nobody's told me that? 'Cause all of these good-willed and good-hearted people are full of it! That's why!"

"Gem—"

"Listen, let's just get out of this car and get this over with." I hopped out and slammed the door behind me.

"All right, Gem," Ms. Thomas said, getting out of the car. "Let's go."

"Yeah, let's."

I stormed up the brick stairs that led to the front door and rang the bell. A few seconds later, Cousin Crazy appeared.

"Well, looka here, looka here." Cousin Shake smacked his lips, and then took a long and loud suck on his toothpick. "We just finished filling out a milk carton application for you."

"Whatever." I grimaced.

"Baby-Tot-Tot," Cousin Shake yelled over his shoulder.

"Yeah, Cousin Shake," Malik answered from the distance.

"I got some good news for you!"

"What's that?"

"Kunta's back."

4

I could barely eat, and not because I wasn't hungry. But…
because this whole deal pissed me off, and as everyone
sat around the kitchen table enjoying breakfast and each
other's conversation, I was on edge.

I eyed everyone at the table. Along with Ms. Grier and
her husband were Ms. Minnie, Cousin Shake, and Ms.
Grier's real kids, Man-Man and Toi, who were deep in a
conversation. Seated in a high chair next to Toi was a
baby—I think it was hers.

I stared at Malik and hated that he acted as if he be-
longed here. He looked at me and smiled and I shot him
the screw face. He turned away, ate a few pieces of his
dripping pancake. Then he moved on to licking the pancake syrup off of his fingers.

"Why are you eating like that?" I eyed him.

"'Cause it's good." He reached for the tray of bacon
and I met his hand with a slap across his fingers.

I spazzed. "You've had enough!" I pushed the tray of bacon away from him.

"Don't hit him again," Ms. Grier said with an edge.

"Lady, please." I rolled my eyes.

Ms. Grier hesitated. "Gem, I think you should calm down. You don't have to be so defensive."

Whatever.

Ms. Grier handed Malik back the tray of bacon and he hurriedly grabbed a few pieces.

"Slow down, son," Mr. Khalil said to Malik.

"Mr. Khalil, you don't understand. Whenever Gem starts acting like this, it's only a matter of time before we get put out. The caseworker shows up and we gotta roll."

"Nobody's rolling," Ms. Grier said. "Now, let's talk about something positive, please. Man-Man, what are your plans today?"

"I'm chillin'." He stroked the light goatee on his chin and a distant smile ran across his face. "I'ma run up to the mall real quick and see this big butt-tender-lil-cutie—" He paused and looked as if his mind had replayed what he'd just said. He snapped his fingers and pointed. "Yeah. What I meant was that I was going to fill out this job application."

Ms. Grier sipped her coffee. "I thought that's what you meant. And besides, you need to do something other than chase behind those fresh lil nasty skanky girls!"

"Why they gotta be all that, Ma?" Man-Man stuffed a forkful of pancakes in his mouth.

"'Cause that's what you like, birds," Toi snapped. "Pigeons."

Ms. Grier sighed. "Toi, leave your brother alone. And

Man-Man, I'm serious. You and all of these girls are getting out of hand."

"Ma, I told you I got this. And could y'all kill calling me Man-Man?" He popped an invisible collar. "I told you, it's G-Bread, baby."

"What the hell is G-Bread Baby?" Cousin Shake asked.

"Cousin Shake," Man-Man said. "The Bread stands for Money. You know, dough, like dollars."

Cousin Shake shook his head. "Grier, when you gon' get this boy some help?"

Ms. Grier shook her head. "Listen, Man-Man, I want you to take Gem to the mall with you. She needs to get out and see some new things."

"Yo, this isn't a field trip," Man-Man said and then looked over to me. "No offense, but Blockers day was yesterday."

Ms. Grier shot him the evil eye.

"It's cool," I snapped toward Man-Man and then turned to his Mama. "Did I say I wanted to go to the mall with him? Now back up!"

I could tell I'd pushed Ms. Grier's patience to the limit. "Gem, don't speak to me like that—"

"Then stop frontin'! And stop telling my brother what to do. You're not his mother! I got this!"

"I'm the mother of this house!" Ms. Grier said, and as she spoke I could see Cousin Shake's shoulders start to bounce.

"Whatever," I said.

"Gem, it's really no need for you to be so upset," Mr. Khalil added his two cents in.

"And it's *really* no need for you all to be phony!"

"No one's being phony, honey," Ms. Grier tried to assure me.

"And stop calling me honey! You know what? This is just too much for me! I don't need your kids trying to babysit me. I don't need your family trying to turn my brother against me. And I damn sure *don't need* you trying to be my mama!" I rose from the table and stormed out of the kitchen. Once I made it up the stairs, I slammed my bedroom door behind me.

5

"**P**sst, Gem...Ge-emmm...wake-up. Psst, Gem..."
Malik's raspy voice and short, chubby shadow filled my bedroom doorway as he slowly pushed the door open. "Gem-yem-yem-yem..."

I should just lay here and not say a word. Not. One. Word. I was used to Malik waking me up in the middle of the night, but dang his timing sucked. Somehow he always had a way of interrupting my dream at the exact point when Drake was down on one knee and about to ask to marry me.

"Gem," Malik called again.

I sighed. "Yeah, Malik."

"You asleep?"

He can't be serious.... "No, I'm skydiving." I peeked at the clock on my nightstand, which flashed 1 A.M. in vibrant red. I pulled my hot pink sheets up to my neck and turned over.

"You're not skydiving, Gem. You're in the bed, asleep."

Duh!

"Gem," Malik called. "Do you always say crazy things in your sleep? Do you talk in your dreams?"

Kill me.... "Malik, do you have your pillow?" I asked, trying like heck to control the edginess of my tone.

"Yeah."

"Are you sure, 'cause you're not sleeping on mine. You slobber way too much."

"I have my pillow."

"Then stop asking questions and just come on."

"Come on where?"

"Little boy, you better stop playing with me. I already know you're scared—"

"I'm not scared. I'm just not friends with the dark." His bare feet slapped against the floor as he walked over and hopped in my bed. "Could you share the cover?" He tugged on my sheet and that's when I remembered to ask him...

"Did you go to the bathroom before you came in here?"

He hesitated. "Yeah."

I flicked on the lamp next to my bed and a dull yellow light filled the room. "You better not be lying."

"I'm telling the truth. I did use the bathroom."

"Malik, if you pee on me it's gon' be a problem." I flicked the light off.

"I haven't peed in the bed in like a whole week. And why you gotta bring that up?"

" 'Cause I'm tired of waking up and smelling like rotten orange juice." I rolled my eyes at the night.

"Could you stop talking so loud?" Malik said, agitated.

"I'm not talking loud."

"Yes you are."

"Whatever, Malik." I turned over. "I'm going to sleep."

"Wait, I need you to wake me up extra early in the morning."

"Why?" I frowned.

"So everybody can think I slept all night in my bed. I don't want anybody thinking that Baby-Tot-Tot is a punk." He popped the collar of his Power Rangers pajamas. "Baby-Tot-Tot got heart."

"Baby-Tot-Tot is a mess. That whole deal is sooo whack.com."

"No it's not and why you hatin'?"

"Hatin'?" I said, surprised.

"Hater to the fullest."

Oh, no he didn't. "Oh, you getting tough?" I tickled Malik in the center of his stomach. "Don't you ever call me a hater!"

Malik laughed until he cried. "Okay, okay," he chuckled. "I won't call you a hater again."

"You better not." I chuckled and fluffed my pillow under my head. "Now, let's go to sleep."

"Okay," Malik said as I closed my eyes and drifted into my dream world.

I could see Drake clearly. He walked toward me and . . .

"Hey, Gem," Malik tapped me on the shoulder.

My eyes popped open. "What?!" I screamed in aggravation.

"Why are you screaming?"

"Because I'm trying to get my dream on and you keep messing it up!"

"Oh," he said unfazed. "Well, I wanted to tell you that when you ran away I was so scared."

I hesitated. I was all set to tell Malik to shut da eff up and go to sleep, but now I couldn't. "Why were you scared?"

"I thought I would never see you again. I didn't want anybody to hurt you."

"I'm fine, okay?"

"Are you going to run away again?"

"No," I said, unsure.

"Okay." I could hear him smiling.

"Now can we please go back to sleep?" I practically begged.

"Yeah," Malik said as he curled up against me.

"Move over," I said. But instead of Malik moving away, he moved closer.

Whatever. I closed my eyes and drifted back into my lovely dream. *"Yo, Gem,"* I dreamed Drake saying. *"You're the love of my life."*

"I know," I answered back.

"And there's something I've been wanting to ask you." Drake dropped to one knee. *"Will you—"*

"Gem!"

Oh...hell...no...

"Gem," Malik called my name again and I could've strangled him.

"What!" I screamed.

"Calm down, you don't have to yell at me."

Shoot me.... "What...do...you...want...?"

"I don't want you to be mad at me, okay?"

"I'm not mad at you."

"I mean, mad at me after I tell you something."

"Tell me something like what?"

"First say you won't be mad. Promise."

"Malik—"

"Promise," he pressed.

"All right, I won't be mad. I promise."

"From now on I want you to behave and be nice."

"From now on? Behave? Be nice? To who?" I was caught completely off guard.

"To Ms. Grier, Mr. Khalil, M.C. Ole-G—"

"Who is M.C. Ole-G?"

"Cousin Shake."

"You want me to be nice to Cousin Shake? Oh, you can forget that," I said.

"You *have to* be nice to Cousin Shake, Ms. Minnie, Man-Man, Toi, *and* baby Noah."

"And why do I have to be nice to them?"

"Because I kind of like these people," he said.

"You don't even know these people. And I told you about getting attached."

"I do know them..." Malik insisted.

"We just met them the other day."

"Well, I know them a little bit..."

"Just like you knew the people we lived with before we moved here, and the family before that. And before that. And each one of them still made us leave." I hated to burst his bubble, but he needed to understand our circumstances.

"That's because you were mean to them."

What did he say? "*I* was mean? So it was *my* fault?" I couldn't believe he blamed me. "Are you even serious with this?"

"Yeah, I'm serious. The last two times we moved was

your fault. You were being really mean. And I'm tired of moving. I'm always losing my friends, I'm never able to keep my video games because every foster parent makes me leave them, and I don't like it. So I was thinking that you better be nice, because it's time for you to listen to me!"

I couldn't believe this. "First of all, you don't tell me what to do. It's the other way around and these people aren't exactly that nice to me."

"Yes they are, Gem. You're being mean and I'm tired of it. So I'm warning you, get yo mind right."

"Get. My. Mind. Right?" *Where did he get that from?*

"Fa'sho."

"You've been around M.C. Ole-G too long."

"I mean it, Gem. You better be nice."

"And if I'm not?!"

Malik paused, like maybe he didn't expect me to call his bluff. "Well," he paused again. "If you're not nice and they say we have to leave, I'm not going."

What? I sat up in bed and flicked my lamp on. "What? What do you mean you're not going?"

"I'm not going. I don't like not having a home. I want to stay in the same school all year for once. And I don't want to move anymore. So if you're not nice then you'll have to go by yourself." Tears filled his eyes. "And I mean it."

I didn't know what to say. "Malik, go to sleep," was all that would leave my mouth.

"I'm serious, Gem. I mean it."

And I could tell that he meant it. And yeah, I wanted to remind him that we rolled together, not separately. And I wanted to tell him that it really didn't matter either way if I was nice or not because when all was said and done we would still be asked to leave. But for some reason the words fell dead in my mouth before I could spit them out. "Okay, okay," I said. "Whatever you say, Malik."

"So does that mean you're going to be nice?" he asked, excited. "Please say yes."

I hesitated. I hated to make promises. "Yeah. I'll try to be nice."

"Try real hard!" Malik squeezed me as tight as he could. "You da truth, Gem-yem-yem. Da truth."

"Cool, I'm the truth," I said sarcastically. "Now can you puhlease shut up so I can get my dream on?"

6

I sat Indian style in the center of my bed, surfing through cable channels, when this rude lunatic interrupted me. I looked up and stared at her like she was crazy.

Ms. Grier slammed a hand on her hip. "All week long you've been sitting in this room, only coming out when it's dinnertime, like this is jail and you're reporting to mess hall. Constantly keeping to yourself and not talking to anyone. Well, this is a home, okay!"

What the hell... "Okay," I said nonchalantly, secretly hoping that me agreeing would shut her up and send her on her way. But it didn't. Instead, she yelled, "Khalil, where are you?"

"I'm here, Grier," he said like he was just as sick of her as I was. He stepped through my doorway and took a deep breath. Then he placed four extra-large shopping bags from Forever 21, True Religion, Deliah's, and Hollister on my bed. Afterward, he walked out of my room and quickly returned with three sneaker boxes, a pair of Uggs, and two pairs of four-inch stilettos.

Inside, I felt like I was in heaven, but on the outside I maintained the game face that said I was less than impressed. I knew I should've said thank you, but I didn't.

"I helped to pick it, Gem!" Malik said, excited as I noticed his new outfit: a black pair of jeans, a football jersey, and black pair of Vans. Obviously, he'd been hanging with them at the mall. "This is yours, too, Gem!" He placed a brand new, hot pink, Spalding basketball next to me and whispered, loudly, "She made me do it."

Ms. Grier shot him a look out the corner of her eye.

Malik carried on, "I had to tell her what you liked or it was gon' be a problem."

"I'm sure, Malik," I said.

He continued his loud whisper. "All I told her is that you were a pink Nike girl, who used to shoot hoops."

"You can stop trying to whisper, Malik," I said.

"If I stop whispering then she'll know all your secrets." He squinted. "And I know you don't want anybody to know how good you used to be before you transferred from school to school. And how you used to be the starting point guard and how you'd won a trophy—that we lost somewhere along the way. And I know you don't want her to find out that when you grow up you want to play in the WNBA."

"No, Malik," I said sarcastically. "That's our secret."

"Exactly." He shot me a quick smile and then looked at Ms. Grier. "See, I told you Gem would like the basketball." He turned back to me and said tight-lipped, "Just roll with it. Baby Tot-Tot got you."

"I see," I said sarcastically.

He shot me a quick smile and then looked at Ms. Grier. "See, I told you Gem would like the ball." He turned back to me and said tight-lipped, "Now tell her you like it."

But I couldn't tell her that, because honestly, I was done with balling and I was doing my best to shake any and all urges that I got to play again. That part of my life was dead. I was over it. Mostly because I'd had enough of making a name for myself on a team and then as soon as I got settled in, I'd have to move from one foster home to the next, and the next, and be transferred from one high school to another...and another. So in order to keep my feelings in check, I quit. Never mind that playing ball was the only escape I had. The only worry-free zone in my life... I had to skip all of that and fast-forward to my reality—which had no room for three-point plays.

"Tell her you like it, Gem." Malik repeated, like he was holding his breath until I said yes.

I hesitated. *Just say it.* "Yeah, I like it, it's cool."

"Great," Ms. Grier said. "And maybe when school starts you'll try out for the team."

I wish she would step off.

Ms. Grier paused for a moment and the room grew silent. "Now all we need is a thank you, and we can be on our way," she said, breaking the monotony.

She was really pushing it. "Thank you," I said dryly.

"You're welcome." She smiled as if she'd just struck it rich. "Now, come on Khalil. 'Cause now I need to go to the grocery store."

"The grocery store? Wait for me!" Malik ran after them, leaving me sitting quietly in a sea of department store shopping bags and a basketball.

I told myself that this wasn't a big deal—that it meant absolutely nothing.

Problem was: it felt like a big deal.

And it felt like it meant something...

I shook off my thoughts and peeked into each shopping bag. There were at least eight or nine pairs of jeans, leggings, sweatpants, hoodies, skirts, the cutest T-shirts, blouses, and accessories. Even cute bras and underwear. A heated wave of happiness—that I hadn't felt in a long time—washed over me.

I ran my fingers over the basketball's ridges and through the grooves. A smile forced its way on my face.

I twirled the ball around on the tip of my index finger.

Maybe I don't have anything to lose...

And maybe I do...

Chance it.

I eased off the bed, ball in hand, and walked down the hall toward Man-Man's room.

I bit the corner of my lip and sucked in a deep breath. I swallowed and knocked softly on the door.

"Ma," Man-Man said. "I'm cleaning up my room now. And no, I don't need your help because all you gon' do is stand in the middle of the floor and tell me how this don't make no sense."

I knocked again. "Man-Man," I called.

He hesitated and then I heard him walk toward the door. From the sound of things he unlocked about three deadbolts and knocked off a security chain before he cracked open the door. He pressed his face into the slit and said, "No guns allowed."

"Funny." I twisted my lips to the side. "I wanted to ask you something."

"Whatever you heard, it's not true," he said. "This house is filled with haters and they stay lying on me."

This dude is nuts. "I only wanted to ask you to play ball."

He opened his door wide. "Play ball with who?" He looked down one end of the hallway and then turned his head and looked down the other end.

I placed one hand on my hip. "With me."

"Play ball with you?" He frowned.

"What, you don't play with girls?"

"Nah, I don't. And I especially don't roll with pink balls."

"What, your skills shaky?"

"Gurl, who you think you talking to?" He squared his shoulders and pointed to his chest. "This is G-Bread, the pimp formerly known as Man-Man. I got skills. Mad skills. I just don't ball with chicks."

I rolled my eyes. "You must be scared."

"Never."

"Well then prove it. 'Cause I got twenty bills that says I can play better than you."

"Twenty bills?" His eyes opened wide and he stroked his goatee.

I knew that would get his attention.

"You got twenty dollars?" he asked, raising one brow and dipping the other.

Puhlease. I'm broker than an old ho with no stroll. "Is that a yes?" I asked. "Or you procrastinating?"

Man-Man cleared his throat. "G-Bread never procrasti-nates."

"Then bring it."

"Brought. Just make sure you have some tissue," he

said as he walked out of his room and I followed him out the front door.

"Tissue for what?" I asked as we stepped over toward the basketball hoop.

"For when I spank dat, you'll have something to wipe your tears."

"Boy, please." I flicked my hand and dribbled the ball. "First of twenty."

"Nah, first of ten. You need to pay me two dollars for each shot."

"Oh, you're real cocky."

"I'm not cocky, baby. Confident."

"Whatever." I chuckled as I bounced the ball to him. "Check."

7

"Yo, that lil raggedy pink ball wrecked my flow," Man-Man insisted as he sucked in and shoved out two deep breaths while he rested his hands on his knees.

I bucked my eyes at him and shot him a look that clearly said, *"You buggin'."* "There was no flow. And with all those playground jump shots you tried, you probably wrecked my ball."

"A grown man shouldn't be playing with a pink ball anyway."

A grown man...?

He carried on, "Got me looking all thirsty and everything."

"Thirsty?"

"Yeah, thirsty." He stood up straight and placed his hands over his eyes like a sun visor. "And I hope the neighbors aren't watching me. This better not end up on YouTube."

Is he fa' real? "YouTube?" I couldn't help but laugh.

"You better recognize. Just like er'body wanna Doughie, well er'body want a piece of G-Bread."

What?

"It's my curse," he said proudly. "Every time I turn around, it's a chick sweatin' me 'cause she can't get enough of me. I keep telling 'em it's only one of me, and on my days off she gon' have to kick it with her boyfriend."

He is really feeling himself.

"That's why I had to change my name from Man-Man to G-Bread."

"And what does the G stand for?"

"It stands for Girls can't get enough of genuine fine." He broke out into the end-zone dance and I knew at this moment he was definitely related to Cousin Shake. "And the crowd went wild!" he carried on.

"Umm…" I hesitated, completely lost for words.

"Got you speechless, huh? Playa-playa, baby. That's how I do it."

I blinked not once, but three times. "Oh…kay, so let's just stick to the money you owe me."

Man-Man looked at me and frowned—his laugh lines sank like parentheses around his mouth. "Everything is about money with you too, huh. You just like Toi. I thought having two sisters was hard, and now I got three of 'em. I feel like somebody's trying to kill me."

I paused for a moment.

Did he just call me his sister? And the word foster wasn't in front of it?

"Besides, I'm kind of glad you won," Man-Man continued.

"Yeah, right."

"No, I am. Because now you can spot me some cash when we head out to this party tonight."

"Spot you?"

He draped his left arm over my shoulders. "Check it, lil sister—"

There it was again...

"Picture it," he pointed to the sky. "Tonight, me and you, at the hottest end-of-the summer-and-back-to-school-jammy-jam ever! Courtesy of tore-up-in-the-face-but-brickhouse-n-the-waist Shaquita and her twin sister, anybody-can-get-up-in-them-jeans Bownita."

"Sounds like a strip club."

"Nah, these are respectable church-going girls. Both of 'em sing in the choir. Now, just stay with me. The music is bumpin', and then I walk up in the spot with you. Yo, you know how much play that's gon' get me with the honeys?"

"No."

"Check it, they gon' look at me and be like 'Look at G.'" Man-Man kicked his voice up at least three octaves. "'G is so hot and understanding. He brought his lil sister out the house and to the club. He's so sweet and sensitive. I love him.'"

"Oh, so, this is only for your benefit?"

His voice returned to normal. "Nah, we gon' both have fun. Lots of it."

"Well, all of that would be nice if I really had some money, but I don't." I walked toward the front door and by the time I reached the doorway, I noticed Man-Man wasn't behind me. I turned around and don't you know this clown had the nerve to look shocked.

He stuttered, "What you, what you, what you mean you

don't have any money? What happened to it? How you gon' make a bet and don't have any money?"

"Excuse you?"

"I don't believe this."

"Believe it." I walked into the foyer and toward the stairs.

"Hold up." He jogged behind me. I stopped and stood on the bottom step. "A'ight," he paused. "A'ight, let's re-group." He tapped his left index finger against his temple. "It's coming to me." He snapped his fingers. "It's coming to me.... A'ight, boom, this is what we gon' do. You gon' hit up Mommy for some money *and* her car. 'Cause I don't have any gas in mine."

Rewind... "What?!"

"She'll give it to you," he said reassuringly as he patted me on my right shoulder.

"First of all, I can't drive."

"I can. Got a license and everything."

"Then why can't you ask?"

"Because Toi murdered my reputation around here. I need to lay back in the cut for a minute. Feel me? But I know exactly what you could say."

"I can't ask Ms. Grier for money. And I'm definitely not asking for the car. Boy, please." *Was he crazy?*

"Whatcha mean you can't ask?" His eyes popped out. "So you gon' do me dirty like that?"

"This isn't about you. I'm just not doing it."

"A'ight," he turned to walk away, but quickly turned back around. "A'ight," he said and shrugged his shoulders. "It's cool. So, umm, I guess we'll have to stay home and watch Cousin Shake chase Ms. Minnie around the house."

"Keep my name outcha mouth!" Cousin Shake spat as

he walked past us wearing the tightest and the nastiest pair of red and blue Superman underwear I'd ever seen. And to top it off, he had on taxi-cab yellow knee pads and a clear plastic cape tied around his neck!

Gagging...

Immediately, I leaned against the wall because I knew that at any moment I would have a flashback of seeing Cousin Shake practically naked and die.

Jesus take the wheel...

"Told you." Man-Man looked me over. "Can't breathe, can you? Now, the choice is yours. So, what you gon' do?"

I cleared my throat and stood up as straight as I could. "So how exactly should I ask her?"

8

I've never been into fashion.
Never been stuck up.

A diva wannabe.

Never thought that I was the flyest chick who'd ever lived...

But tonight was different.

Because when I walked up in the spot, I straight shut it down.

Freeze!

Pow!

Ka-boom!

Gem has stepped in the room.

I felt like I was sashaying on clouds—or better, the red carpet. All eyes were on me like the paparazzi and for the first time in my life I loved the attention.

Why?

Because I didn't have to cuss, fight, scream, or demand anything to get it. All I had to be was me: a cute mocha brown chick with thick size ten hips, a sexy shoulder length ponytail, and a swoop bang dipped low over my right eyebrow. I rocked a black camisole, a black bandage miniskirt, four-inch hot pink stilettos, hoop earrings, and sparkling bangles adorned my right arm.

Hotness.com described me perfectly.

"Dang, girl," Man-Man shot me a sly grin as we stood near the doorway. "The whole place just dropped the mic."

"I know, right." I laughed a little as my eyes skipped around the dimly lit and extra-large living and dining room combination. The place was packed with girls and hotties who lined the walls and filled the floor, some dancing and others kicking it.

Tucked in the far left corner of the living room was a makeshift bar of soda, fruit punch (which, judging from the way everybody hovered over it, I'm sure was spiked), and Shirley Temples made to order for a dollar a cup. Next to the bar was the D.J., who from the moment I walked in had been fiyah. He mixed Rihanna and Chris Brown's "Cake" and Big Sean's "Dance" and bumped it through his mega speakers like crazy.

For a split second a tizzy of nervousness invaded my stomach. In an attempt to shake it off, or at least play it off, I leaned from one foot to the next, while Man-Man looked as if he was a king admiring his court. "I knew they would drop the mic, though. They always do," he said.

"Oh, really?"

"Yeah, they can't help it."

"And why not?"

" 'Cause girls love Genuine Fine." He looked to his right, stroked his goatee, and pointed at a duo of chicks standing a few inches away from him. "I see you," he said, and the girls turned fever red and broke out into stupid giggles.

"Hey G," the boldest one said as the other one gave him a shy wave while looking away.

Man-Man looked at me and shook his head. "My entourage. They're addicted to me."

Hang me.

"I'ma start a G-world support group," Man-Man carried on.

This dude was super corny—but funny—but corny. And he was kind of cute in a brotherly sort of way: five eleven, brown sugar-colored skin, a close and cropped hair cut, and a wide smile that made all the girls think he was admiring them when he was really admiring how well his ridiculous lines worked on them.

I snapped my fingers. "That's right, it's all about you. What was I thinking?" I twisted my lips and rolled my eyes. *Puhlease.*

"It's in the genes, girl. It's in the genes." He turned his head from side to side and then looked straight. "Now come on and beat your feet to the bar. 'Cause you need to be buying a drink right about now."

What? "Excuse you?" I looked at him like he was loco. "I'm not one of your groupies so you can't order me to buy a drink. And besides, I don't want a drink right now."

"What did I just tell you to do," he mumbled.

"Excuse you?!" I shot back. "I should know if I want a drink or not."

"Why can't you just follow my lead?" he whispered.

"Because I don't have to."

"But I need you to."

"Why?"

"See those chicks over there?" He nodded across the room toward a clique of three girls who stared me down like I'd just robbed 'em on the playground.

"Yeah, I see 'em. And?"

"And the one in the middle is Coca-Cola curves, Cameron. Just look at her." He squinted his eyes and bit into his bottom lip. "That body is poppin' in *all* the right places. That's her nickname, too. Pop-Pop."

Oh, my God . . .

The conceit continued. "She likes me. Texts me all day. Always on my Facebook, tweets love songs to me. I'm always on her mind."

"Oh, wow, I betchu the day she met you is now a holiday."

He pointed from my eyes to his and back again. "Now you're following me."

I shook my head. "You are really feeling yourself."

"No, I'm not. I'm humble on Saturday . . . or is that Sunday?"

I paused. I didn't even know what to say to that, so I simply moved on. "So, do you like her?"

"Heck yeah. I'm diggin' them curves, I mean her mind. I just love the way she thinks."

Yeah right. "So then stop ordering *me* around and go over there and make *her* buy a drink."

"What?" He looked at me like I'd just slapped him. "I'm not running up on no chick." He frowned. "Not even close to how I get down."

"You just said you liked her." I was clearly confused.

"I do like her. As a matter of fact, I've made her my girl a few times. Which is exactly why I have to make her sweat even more than all the other girls around here lusting after me."

"Speechless."

"Now see, if you get a drink, she gon' think we're together, then she gon' get all worked up—a little wrinkle will form on her nose and tears will glisten in her eyes— and that's gon' allow me to slide my arms around her waist and be like, this my new sister, girl. Chill."

"Something...is...really wrong with you..."

Man-Man completely ignored me. Instead, he stared off in deep thought, flicked the toothpick from the right corner of his mouth to the left and as if a lightbulb had gone off, he said, "Know what, skip the drink. That was a whack idea."

"I'm glad we agree."

"I got one even better." He popped the invisible collar of his red Young Money T-shirt and slid his right hand in the side pocket of his True Religion jeans. "Follow me," he said like his name should've been Cat Daddy.

I stood back and watched Man-Man get his serious pimp stroll on: leaning slightly to the right while one shoulder dipped in front of the other. He stopped for a moment and looked back at me. "Come on."

I followed him, reluctantly, because judging from the way the groupies he glided toward continued to stare at me, it was about to go down. Seriously.

The closer we got to the desperate-in-the-city clique, the madder Coca-Cola and her crew looked. They each placed their hands on their hips, their necks seemed frozen in a twisted to the left position, and their bottom lips hung like a horse's.

They each rolled their eyes at me in slow motion and I gave them a look that invited them to bring it; that's when I noticed that Man-Man had stretched his arms forward and parted their circle. "Coming through." He pimped his way through the bird's nest and over to a group of dudes standing behind them.

Stop the press...He. Did. Not. Just play them like that. "That was so rude," I mumbled and either Man-Man didn't hear me or chose to ignore me because instead of responding, he gave the guys he'd walked over to pounds, and never once looked back.

But I looked back and for a moment I found myself staring at Coca-Cola. She looked familiar and I knew I'd seen her before, I just didn't know where...

"And why is she eye-slicing you?" one of Coca-Cola's friends spat, snapping me out of my gaze. Now, had I been on the street I would've straight stepped to 'em, but since none of this was really my problem and tonight's mission was to have a good time, I turned away from them. My intention was to keep it movin'—but then one of Coca-Cola's friends lost her mind and said, "Who's this ho?" Which halted my mission and required my immediate attention.

I spun around and Coca-Cola looked me dead in my eyes and said, "Yeah, that's what I wanna know. Who's the ho?"

Breathe...Breathe...now check 'em. I shot this clique a fake Barbie smile. "Clearly you can see that he doesn't do hoes, because he left you standing there." I pointed my hands like guns and pulled the triggers. "Click, click, boom!"

"I know you not gon' take that!" one of Coca-Cola's friends said to her. "I know you're not going to let her punk you!"

Before Coca-Cola could respond, I said, "Maybe you're not that stupid after all. 'Cause that's exactly what she's going to do! And you too!"

"Whoa, you don't need to be arguing over me." Man-Man slid in between us. "Kamani, relax," he said to Coca-Cola's friend.

I snapped at Man-Man and pointed over his shoulder. "You better get 'em, 'cause they don't want it over here."

"Chill," he said to me as if he was about to choke on laughter. He turned toward Coca-Cola and said with a smooth edge to his voice, "No need to be jealous."

"Jealous!" Coca-Cola snaked her neck, paused, then snaked her neck again.

"Oh, he got you twisted," Kamani said to Coca-Cola as her eyes taxied over me, which was cool, because one thing I wasn't was scared. Ever.

"You're welcome to bring it," I said to Kamani and I stepped to the side of Man-Man. "The only thing separating us is air and opportunity! As a matter of fact, let me do you a favor and warn you. If you step to me you gon' need to bring King Kong with you." I turned to Man-Man, whose cheeks were stuck on blushed. "You think this is cool? Really? You better get these birds before I clip their wings."

"Pop," Man-Man shook his head. "Kamani, Janay chill. This is my lil sister."

Coca-Cola blinked her extended lashes as if they were battery operated. Once her batteries died, she stopped blinking and her eyes popped open. "You must think I'm stupid."

"Duh," Kamani butted in. "It's obvious he thinks you're stupid. 'Cause he expects you to believe that two weeks ago he had two sisters and now suddenly it's three!"

"Exactly," Man-Man said as if this type of thing happened every day.

"Exactly, what?" Coca-Cola asked. "You think I'm stupid?"

"No!" Man-Man waved his hands. "I meant *exactly* I had two sisters two weeks ago and now I have three."

"Whatever." Kamani carried on, "I keep telling you, you need to check him."

It was obvious that Coca-Cola was mad, but her friend was hyping her up so much that I just had to step back in. So I said, "Why don't you mind your business! Or are you too jealous to do that?" I looked at their other homegirl who hadn't opened her mouth and said, "You better get this chick and tell her to fall in line."

Homegirl didn't say a word.

"G!" Coca-Cola screamed. "Why are you trying to play me crazy! Don't try me, G. 'Cause I will turn this whole party out!"

"Pop," he softly cupped her chin. "I'm touched that you would wreck shop over me, but I can't let you tear up the spot."

"You know what, Pop," Kamani snapped. "You can deal with him in a minute, but first you need to handle this trick." She turned to me.

I retorted, "Well since you're all in the business, why don't you do it!"

Kamani sucked her teeth. "What you better do—!"

"All I *better* do," I said, "is stay cute. Anything else is my choice!"

"You got me messed up!"

" 'Cause that's what you are, a mess!"

"Kamani," Man-Man butted in. "Chill, I told you this is really my sister. She's been my sister for about two weeks!"

"Wait a minute," Coca-Cola said and squinted at me. "Don't I know you?"

"You don't know me," I snapped. "But you can." I took a step forward.

"No, for real," she said, changing her tone from ready to leap across the room to calm.

Yeah, hella crazy.

Coca-Cola looked as if she searched my face for an answer. "Is your name Gem? Gem Scott?"

Pause... what? Before I could say anything, she continued.

"That's your name, right?" she asked as if she really needed me to say yes.

"Oh, you know this chick?!" Kamani said. "That's even worse!"

I shook my head. "Look, I don't know what the heck is really going on here. But I don't do drama or crazy. I just came to chill. Now this is my brother—take it or leave it. But I don't want him like that. He's all yours, boo-boo." I looked at Man-Man and rolled my eyes. "Now I need a drink."

I stepped away and left them all behind me. I'd made up my mind that when we got home I would be taking Man-Man and chopping him dead in his throat. By the time I reached the bar, Coca-Cola was in my face again. "Seriously. For real," she said. "No beef. But can you please tell me if your name is Gem Scott?"

I was straight aggravated and I didn't know if I was aggravated more because this girl knew my name or that she wouldn't step off.

"Do you have a little brother named Malik?" she continued to pry.

How does she know that?

"Do you?" she asked for confirmation.

"Why are you all in my business?"

"Because you look just like my best friend."

"Okay, and, clearly you can see that I'm not your bestie."

"But you could be. I haven't seen her since I was like twelve. We lost contact and she looked exactly like you. Her name was Gem and she and her little brother, Malik, used to live with my grandmother. She was their foster mother. But when she died they moved and I don't know what happened to them." Tears glimmered in her eyes. "And for a minute I thought maybe you were her."

I didn't say anything, mostly because I didn't know what to say. Especially since I now knew exactly who she was: Cameron "Popcorn" Hunter. Everybody called her Popcorn because that's all she ever wanted to eat.

Her grandmother, Ms. Betty, was my foster mother and Popcorn used to come over her house every day. That's how we became best friends.

We went to school together, were in the same class, and swore we were the only two girls in the world who could step—I mean really bring it.

When Popcorn had her first boyfriend in sixth grade

and I didn't have one, we created a club with only the two of us and called it the Rich Girlz. Why? 'Cause that's what we both wanted to be—rich. And our club had only one rule: No boyz were allowed to come between our friendship. So when her boo got jealous, she dumped him.

We thought we had it all figured out—but then her grandmother died—and we didn't know how to resolve that. So in the blink of an eye our lives changed.

Malik and I returned to being gypsies and Popcorn and I lost contact.

"Okay," she swallowed and dapped at the corner of her right eye. "It's cool, I guess I was mistaken." She turned to walk away.

"It's me," I said dryly, not knowing exactly how to react.

She turned back around and her eyes lit up. "For real—for real? Or for real just so I won't think I'm crazy, have an emotional breakdown, go home and eat all the popcorn I can get my hands on."

I tried not to smile, but I couldn't help it. "Nacho cheese with hot sauce."

"And a little bit of salt, pepper—"

"And globs of butter." I cracked up. "The only kind you would eat when you were mad."

"My edible boyfriend." She smiled like a kid who'd been given free candy. "So it's really you, Gem?"

"The one and only!"

"I can't believe this!" she squealed, and we embraced. For a moment I wasn't certain if this was weird or simply perfect. But one thing I knew for sure, I felt like I was hugging the best part of my life.

"The original Rich Girlz are back together again! We can't lose touch, ever!" she said. Her voice was high-pitched, squeaky, and she spoke a mile a minute—the same way she did when we were twelve.

"We won't," I said.

"I can't believe this!" She smiled. "Girl, I'm surprised you didn't remember me when G was calling me Pop."

"Well, I thought he was calling you Pop because...well he said..." I hesitated. I started to sell Man-Man out, considering the havoc he caused, but then I changed my mind. "I guess I just didn't put two and two together. And plus he never called you Popcorn."

"Yeah, as I got older the nickname became shorter." She smiled and playfully pushed me on my shoulder. "I just can't believe—"

"All right listen," Man-Man's voice boomed as he found his way from across the room and into our conversation. "All of this arguing has to end. I thought y'all were over here hugging it out, but now I see you're about box over me again." He stood in between us and draped an arm over each of our shoulders. "I'm a playboy not a fire-fighter. And Pop this is really my sister. So I need you to calm down. You know it's a G-world girl and you're the only bird I want in my tree."

"Boy, please." Pop pushed Man-Man's arm off of her shoulder. "I didn't forget how you just tried to play me."

"Don't be like that, Pop." He turned toward me. "Tell her, Gem."

"It's a G-world, you handle it," I said.

Pop looked at me and smiled. "Come on, girlie, let's go get our dance on!"

"Yeah, let's," I said as we walked away holding hands, our stilettos making drum beats behind us.

"Pop!" Man-Man screamed. "I was just playing, and why y'all holding hands?"

We didn't answer we just kept it movin'.

Man-Man continued, "Gem, Pop, please don't tell me y'all ordering fish-filet. I didn't mean to hurt you that bad!"

"He is out of control," I said.

"Yeah, he is." Pop blushed and squealed, bumping against my arm. "But he's *soooo* freakin' cute."

9

"*Girrrlzzzz, drop it to the flooooor…!*" Waka Flocka Flame's "No Hands" blasted through the D.J.'s speakers, as he mixed in the toughest bass beat I'd ever heard. The music alone took this party to a whole other level—transmitting everyone to another zone. Hands were in the air and everybody bounced, rocked, and shouted in unison, "Look, ma, no hands…!"

I was so caught up and lost in the moment that for the first time ever since I'd been on my own I didn't think about my mother never getting herself together or where I'd lay my head next. The only thing on my mind was having a good time.

"Look, ma, no hands…!" The crowd shouted and bounced as if we were in a stepper's dance.

"The twins know their parties be crazy!" Pop fanned her face as the D.J. slowed the music down to Beyoncé's "Rather Die Young" and mostly everyone on the floor coupled up. Unless of course, you were solo, a third wheel, or came with your friends—then you stepped to the side or headed to the bar.

Me and Pop chose the bar.

We ordered two Shirley Temples and nodded our heads to the mellow beat. "We have so much to catch up on," Pop said, as she played with the tip of her stirrer. "Like, I need to tell you about all my boos since sixth grade. And how out of all of them I thought G was going to be the one, but I'm so done with him."

I twisted my lips so far to the left that the right side of my mouth sank. "You need to stop," I said, not believing a word she'd said. Especially since Man-Man stared at her and she couldn't sip her drink for smiling at him.

"I'm serious," she insisted and turned her head away from him. Pop pushed her hair behind her ears and her lime green feather earrings dangled on her shoulders. "I'ma just be by myself for a while and G can do what he wants to do. See who he wants to see, 'cause I'ma do me."

I sipped my drink. "Sure."

"You don't believe me?"

"Umm, no."

"And why not?" She looked hurt.

"For one you keep staring at him."

"My eyes can't help it. I'm addicted to cuties." She peeked over at Man-Man and the moment he looked up and over at her she turned back to me. "He is so fine." Her eyes rolled up to the ceiling, she stared off into a daze, and then regained her focus. "But he is not the only fine fish in the sea. 'Cause this is not just G's world, this is Popcorn's world too, you feel me?"

"I hear you."

"G is always trying to play me like I'm some jealous lunatic. Which, I'm not. I'm just passionate about my feelings."

"Okay." I took another sip.

"Girl," she looked at her watch. "It's 12:32 and by 12:37, I'ma be so over that boy it'll be a shame."

"Wow, five minutes. That must be a record."

"It might be. But hmph, I'ma ballplayer, not a chaser." She put up her hand for a high-five.

"Okay!" I slapped my hand against hers.

"Boom." She turned back around and looked over at Man-Man. "You think I'm beat by that girl all...up...in... his face? Well, I'm not."

"Umm hmm."

Pop paused, squinted. "Hmph, it's like she's trying to swallow his breath they're so close. She's smacked and smashed all up in his grill."

"Dead in it."

She placed her hands over her eyes like a sun-visor. "Like she could eat him for breakfast, lunch, dinner—"

"And a snack," I added. "But you're not beat for that."

"Not sweatin' it one drop." Pop squinted again. "But she really needs to back up. Wait, is that Janay?" Her eyes popped open. "Oh hold up, wait a minute. I'm 'bout to put some push up in it." She snaked her neck, paused, and snaked it again. "Has she lost her mind?"

"That's the quiet chick you were with earlier, right?" I asked.

"Yeah."

"Maybe she was just looking for you." I shrugged.

"Well, I'm over here, boo." She snapped her fingers. "You know, I'm like 5' 7", size twelve, you can't miss me.

She doesn't need to be in G's face looking for me. Plus I have to keep an eye on Janay anyway."

"Why?"

"'Cause she's quiet and my grandma always said you have to watch the quiet ones. Plus, when she smiles at G her grin is more than one eighth of an inch."

Now that caught me completely off guard. "More than one what?"

"One eighth of an inch. That's how wide her smile should be when she's looking at G."

"Why?"

"Because that's a nice-and-friendly respectful you're-my-friend's-boo-type-of smile. But Janay hits G with a smile so wide a truck could drive through it. And that's a sneaky smile. A smile that clearly says when my friend's back is turned, I'll be trying to side bag her boo."

"Wow."

"And that's against *all* the rules! Plus, I don't play that."

"Maybe it's nothing shady. Maybe she really was looking for you and didn't see you. Pop, it is a lot of people in here."

"Well, if she didn't see me, she's about to. And if it looks shady and Janay got that side-bagging smile on her face, then this party is about to be a beat-down crime scene." She marched toward Man-Man and I walked alongside of her. "I ain't the one," she announced.

"Let's just hear what she has to say first, and anyway didn't you just say you were done with him?"

"So what? I don't need her cleaning up after me. Suppose I want seconds? And besides it's not 12:37, it's 12:36 and I still have a whole minute to lose it!" Pop stormed in between Man-Man and Janay. She turned toward Janay and said, "And what's this about?"

Janay's smile was nervous but wide—straight deer caught in headlights.

Before they could say anything, Pop stepped into Janay's personal space. "I know you're not trying to be a homewrecking-homie-hop?!"

A what?

"No, girl," she said, as if they actually understood what a homewrecking-homie-hop was.

"I was over here because Kamani sent me to look for you," Janay said.

"For what?" Pop snarled.

"'Cause we wanted to go and get something to drink." Janay hesitated.

"Well, I'm not thirsty," Pop said, sarcastically. "But since you are, then you better get on."

"Whatever," Janay said, as she hurried out of Pop's way. Once she was out of eyesight Man-Man smiled from ear to ear and said to Pop, "It wasn't even like that. As soon as Janay started smiling I told her to close her mouth."

"Don't try me, G."

"Look at you," he carried on, proudly. "Getting all mad. I just love it when you get that wrinkle in your nose."

Pop fought back a blush and rolled her eyes. "Mad? Puhlease. I ain't mad!" she carried on but I could no longer focus on what she was saying, because something—or better *someone*—across the room had just snatched my attention away.

I thought about turning away, but I couldn't. I felt forced to look straight ahead and stare. I couldn't help it.

The cutie who stood across the room from me was soooo fine—that all I could think was *goddamn*. . . .

He was 6' 2", wore a navy-blue Yankees snap back bent like a half a moon over his chestnut-colored eyes. His skin was the color of a Hershey's Kiss, and his right arm was covered with a colorful tattoo sleeve. Sexy. And his gear was on point: slightly baggy skinny-jeans, a blue and white plaid button up, with the sleeves pushed over his elbows, and crisp white Jordans on his feet.

As if on cue the D.J. played Monica's "Anything (to Find You)" and he walked toward me.

My stomach did four flips. I diverted my eyes from him and turned to the side.

Breathe in . . .

Breathe out . . .

And chill . . .

I turned back around and like a flash of light he'd disappeared.

My heart jumped.

"Gem." Pop called my name as if she'd been calling me for a minute.

I felt like I'd been in space. "Yeah?"

Pop pointed to the middle of the living room floor where couples slow danced. "Me and G decided we couldn't live without each other so we're going over here to celebrate."

And before I could protest, say okay, or even ask her what she'd just said to me, they were already in the middle of the floor wrapped in each other's arms, leaving me to wonder if I'd just gone crazy.

I did my best to shake off my thoughts as I walked back

toward the bar, glanced over my shoulder, and thought that maybe...

Know what, I'm trippin'...

I placed my dollar on the bar, reached for my drink, and leaned against the wall.

"Praying to see me," drifted into my ears.

I opened my eyes, swallowed, and fought with everything in me not to smile, but nothing stopped my eyes from dancing in delight. The corners of my lips crept their way toward a smile, but I managed to keep them turned down as I said, "Am I praying to see you? Not at all." I sipped my drink. "But what I did pray, is that you weren't stalking me."

Why did I say that?

He smirked—a sexy smirk—but a smirk nonetheless... then he looked me over, leaned in, and stroked the right side of my face from my cheek to my chin. "Trust me, I'ma lot of things, Pretty Girl, but one thing I'm not is a stalker."

"And how would I know that?"

Oh...my...God...Just when I thought I couldn't get any dumber, my mouth sinks to an all-new low.

I smiled, hoping that my cuteness would somehow erase his memory of what I'd just said.

My heart thundered loudly and I wondered if he could hear it. I swear all of this was new to me.

I sipped my drink and he smirked.

This whole deal was going south real quick.

"Know what? You're way too beautiful for your mouth to be so slick. And maybe the next time a dude tries to kick it to you, you'll have your mind right." He hit me with a two-finger peace sign and left.

Did he just call me crazy?
I swallowed.
Watched him disappear into the crowd.
Maybe I shouldn't have...

"Everybody on the floor...!" Ciara's throwback "1, 2 Step" blasted through the D.J.'s speakers and I joined the line dance. A few minutes into it—and although I knew every step—from watching the video over and over again—my rhythm was off. And the last thing I wanted was to look stupid, again.

I gave up the dance and headed toward the bathroom. Of course there was a line—which I had no patience for. I decided to wait, and not because I had to use it, but because I wanted a moment alone. Scratch that, I needed a moment alone.

The line moved hella slow.

I opened my clutch purse and took out my compact.

Lips...still poppin'.

Eyes...revealed too many thoughts that I didn't want to deal with.

I quickly put the mirror away and continued to wait. But after a while the line seemed permanently on pause, so I gave up and walked away.

This party had gone from a ten to negative one. All I wanted was to go home, crawl in bed, and toss the covers over my head. But at the moment, with Pop and Man-Man crazy-glued to one another I couldn't do that.

I need some fresh air.

I walked toward the front door and as I made my way through the crowd my eyes scanned everyone...just in case...

The night's breeze felt like a relief when I stepped outside on the porch. My heels clicked as I leaned against the black iron stair rail and looked out into the street—only for my eyes to meet him: standing on the street corner beneath a flickering street lamppost, kicking it with a group of his boys.

Be bold.

No. If anything, I need to go back inside.

Just chill and stand here.

I hesitated.

Maybe I should...

Maybe I shouldn't...

I slid a piece of gum in my mouth, blew a minty-fresh bubble, and popped it.

I can't...

This was crazy.

He was too far for me to hear anything more than a few shrieks of laughter that drifted from his conversation but he was close enough for me to see him smile, turn his head, and notice me standing here. We locked gazes for about two point five seconds and then the butterflies took over my stomach and I couldn't take the stare-off anymore.

A few minutes later I looked back in his direction. He was no longer looking this way and had resumed his conversation with his friends. I wondered was he talking about me.

I watched him pull car keys from his pocket.

Is he leaving?

Get it together...

Get it together...

And go over there...

I swallowed.

Just do it…

My heels echoed like wind chimes as I sauntered through my anxiousness and catwalked over to where he and his friends stood.

This was the bravest I'd ever been. Ever.

Relax, relax, and play it cool. My presence immediately brought their conversation to a halt. "Hey." I gave the group of five a small wave. Then I looked directly at my interest and said, "Can I speak to you for a minute?"

Silence. Complete and utter silence for at least two seconds and then he gave each of his boys a pound and said to them. "A'ight, yo, I'll get up with y'all later."

As his friends walked away they each looked at me and smiled. One of them even said to him, "This you?"

He answered, "Maybe."

That response caused me to blush like crazy. I tried to erase it quickly from my face but no matter how hard I tried the blush didn't fade. And suddenly I felt my temperature rise to two hundred degrees.

Jesus…

Dear God, please don't let that be sweat I feel bubbling on my forehead. This is no time to be anti-sexy.

I placed my right hand on my forehead and slyly checked for sweat.

No sweat.

Whew.

I am way too nervous. I need to calm down. I mean, he's cute and all, but it's not that serious.

Yeah right…

Once his boys went their separate ways—some returned to the house party and others left in their cars—he looked at me and said, "Wassup?"

I hesitated and unintentionally ended up swallowing my gum. Dang! "Umm, nothing's up." *Why did I say that? I. Sound. So. Stupid. Let me try this again.* "What I meant was something was up. I mean is up."

I was getting dumber by the moment.

Ugg!

I curled the corners of my lips, which made my dimples bling, and then I said in a soft and playful tone, "So umm, what had happened was I, umm, came over here because I thought you were this cutie that I'd just met at the party."

Please let him play along...please.

"Oh, really." He tilted his head to the side with a slight grin.

Ding!

"Umm hmm." I snapped my fingers for emphasis and he chuckled a bit—not a lot, but enough to let me know I had his attention.

The butterflies in my stomach felt like they were doing the Running Man, but I continued on. "He was tall like you, had eyes like hazel sapphires—just like you, he had the same sleeve of hot tattoos—like you, and his bad boy swag with the good boy edge was like yours, too."

"Oh really." His eyes smiled. "He sounds familiar. I might know him."

"You just might."

He cracked up. Not too much—but just enough to let me know he had a sexy laugh.

He was such a boss.

"So, anywho, since you looked like the dude I thought I would chance it and run over here."

"A'ight, you're here and I'm him. Now what?"

Good question... "Now you tell me your name."

"Hmmm..."

"And not your street name, your government."

He gave me a slanted smile and my heart fluttered.

"Why do you wanna know my government?" he teased. "What are you supposed to be, the police?"

For some reason, him saying that turned me on. "Are you gon' tell me?"

He stepped into my personal space. My nose was a few inches from his collarbone and for a moment, all I wanted to do was take the tip of my index finger and slide it across it. He looked down into my eyes and said. "Ny'eem."

I cheesed. Hard. "Hi, Ny'eem. I'm Gem."

"Nice meeting you, Gem."

"You, too," I said nervously, wondering if my buckling knees would hold up in my stilettos.

"I'd like to see you again, kick it with you sometime."

"Yeah, that would be cool."

"Let me see your cell phone."

I swallowed, nervously handed him my phone. He programmed his number and pressed CALL so that my number would pop up on his phone, then handed the phone back to me and said, "I'll look for you to call me."

"I will," I said and took two steps back. I didn't want to walk away, but I felt a nervous urge to. I blushed. "Later." I waved bye and boldly blew him a kiss.

Just as I'd turned away, Ny'eem called my name, "Gem."

I turned back toward him and he walked up close to me, moving even deeper into my personal space than he was before. "I wanna tell you something," he said.

"What's that?"

"I know we just met and everything, but I wanna kiss you."

Pause. What did he just say? Did I just pass out and have an out of body experience? He wants to what? Kiss me?

"Really?" was all I could think to say and just when I knew I had to be dreaming he said, "Yeah, really."

And he kissed me.

And I kissed him back.

Tongues dancing...

Smoothly...

Slowly...

Gently...

In the soft yellow stream of the flickering street light.

In the shadow of the platinum moon.

We kissed...

And we kissed until his hands embraced my waist, mine slid around his thick neck, and I felt like we were the only two people in the world who existed.

10

Six thirty A.M.

"Rise and grind, super-freaks it's schooltime! And tri-flin' season has officially ended."

Am I having a nightmare...?

Am I...?

"This is my favorite time of the year," Cousin Shake an-nounced proudly as he pounded his fist from my bed-room door, down the hallway, and over to Man-Man's room. "'Cause I'm the Get-Y'all-Azzes-To-School police!"

He snorted and continued, "See, the warm weather runs y'all crazy, and school time is just what I need to rein your lazy behinds back in. All summer long you been run-ning around here gettin' ya derelict on. Man-Man grew a goatee and now he's addicted to hoochies. Gem ran away and had to be carted back by the social-workin'-po-po. Now Baby-Tot-Tot may eat up everything in sight, but he's the best one around here. At least he has some manners. Respectful. Matter-fact, he's the reason y'all are still alive.

He keeps me calm, 'cause I can't stand teenagers. I wanna bust 'em in the chest every chance I get."

O…M…G…

His voice has to be illegal.

I grabbed my pillow and placed it over my head.

"Now get up!" He pounded on my bedroom door again. "'Cause you got three minutes to shower, kill your stank morning breath, and get to school."

Trippin'.

"I'm up, Cousin Shake, dang, man," I heard Man-Man say. He must've been standing right outside my door, because he was close enough for me to hear the aggravation in his voice.

Cousin Shake worked everybody's nerves.

"What you mean 'dang'?" Cousin Shake barked. "Dang is real close to bang. What you a gangsta now? Is that a threat, homie? Huh? Huh?" I may have only been able to hear them, but I knew for sure that Cousin Shake was doing his cat daddy and bounce routine.

Man-Man released a deep and aggravated sigh. "Why you always dancing?"

Knew it.

Man-Man continued, "Don't you have asthma? Didn't you have to go to the emergency room the last time you broke out into a routine?"

"Well this time I'ma take you with me. Now buck," Cousin Shake spat. "I dare you."

"A'ight, a'ight, chill. Take your chest down, I'm going in the bathroom now."

"I thought so." Cousin Shake grimaced. "'Cause you don't want none of this, G-Bread, 'cause that G will be standing for 'Got molly-whopped!' Now say something, 'cause I'm looking for a reason to turn this into beat-down season."

Man-Man didn't respond and when I heard the bathroom door close I knew he'd given up the argument.

Surprisingly everything became quiet. I guess after cussing Man-Man out Cousin Shake forgot about me. Thank God.

I looked at my alarm clock and figured I could steal a few minutes of sleep. I closed my eyes and snuggled into my pillow. And just when my mind filled with a beautiful dream of Drake, shouts of, "Gymnasium!" scared the heck out of me.

I sat straight up in bed and realized Cousin Shake was back to rattling my bedroom door again.

"Get up!" he said.

I tossed the covers off of me, stormed out of bed, and snatched the door open. "I don't need a human alarm clock."

"Well you got one." Cousin Shake gave a sinister grin while his beer belly danced beneath the burgundy robe he had on. He took two steps back and we soaked up a full view of each other.

I had on a pair of gray sweats and a white T-shirt.

Cousin Shake looked like his name was Pookie and he was about to testify in a news interview. He had a floral shower cap on his head, a super-tight robe that fell to his ashy knees, black dress socks—one stretched up his left calf and the other slouched down to his ankle—and on his extra-wide feet were brown corduroy house shoes that he'd broken down in the back by walking on the heels— transforming his house shoes to slip-ons. He grunted,

"Breaka-breaka-one time. You opened that door like you tryna do something."

Suddenly I got a flashback of him dragging me by my neck, so I didn't move and I didn't say anything. Not that I was letting him punk me or anything, I just wasn't in the mood.

"Yeah, I didn't think you wanted it." Cousin Shake looked me over. " 'Cause you know I will make it rain."

Whatever.

Man-Man walked out of the bathroom with a towel wrapped around his waist and one tossed over his shoulder. He looked at me and started doing the Running Man. "Now go on—get in the bathroom," he said, mocking Cousin Shake.

I cracked up and started doing the bounce. "I's a goin'!" I said. "I's a goin'." I bounced and laughed my way into the bathroom, closing the door behind me.

"Yeah," Cousin Shake said. "Y'all can dance all day like you think it's funny, but you already know how I get down. 'Cause Cousin M.C. Shake ain't playin'. So that's right, gon' get in that bathroom! And out of the three minutes you had to shower, Gemini, your nasty mouth has already used up two."

Kick Rocks

I looked at my reflection in the full-length mirror that hung on the back of my closet door.

My hair was pulled into a sleek ponytail.

Eyes were lined.

Lashes were full.

Lips were plump and shiny with cherry-flavored gloss.

My black jeans hugged my curves like a leather glove, my slouchy, yellow, and mid-drift sweatshirt hung off one shoulder, and my matching yellow camisole underneath was real cute. My brown leather stilettos—made like ankle boots with a peep toe—and my gold hoop earrings and bangles topped it all off.

My gear was sick. Extra fly...so why didn't I feel fly? Instead, I felt pissed. Scared. And I had the urge to crawl back into bed and pretend that none of this existed.

This was the third high school I'd been in and I was only a sophomore. Every year I had to start all over again, secretly searching for somewhere to fit in, while acting like it didn't bother me if kids kicked it with me or not—when sometimes...it did.

I hated being the new kid.

Hated it.

But I was always new. Everywhere I went, I was always the last to arrive and the last to fit in...

Always.

At least I had Man-Man, although he was in the eleventh grade, and I had Pop, and thankfully we had homeroom together.

I shook my head and continued to stare at my reflection.

What am I doing?

The one thing I hated more than being the new kid was feeling sorry for myself.

I walked into the kitchen where Toi, Noah, Man-Man, and Malik sat around the table, while Ms. Minnie and Cousin Shake fixed our plates. I sat down and Cousin Shake snapped. "Oh no you didn't just walk in here and not say good morning."

This dude.

Toi took her index finger, swirled it slyly next to her temple, and mouthed, "He's crazy."

I gave a tight smile. "Good morning."

"Now that's better," Ms. Minnie said. "Good mornin', baby."

"Cousin Shake, what are you fussing about?" Ms. Grier said as she walked into the kitchen dressed for work. She smiled at everyone. "I heard you fussing at my children from all the way upstairs." She gave Noah a kiss on the cheek, Malik a kiss on his forehead, and winked her eye at the rest of us.

Cousin Shake shook his head. "Grier, that's why these kids act the way that they do."

"They didn't even do anything," Ms. Grier said.

"They're always doing something. And especially Man-Man."

"Why is it always *especially* me?" Man-Man asked.

"'Cause it's always you," Cousin Shake said. "And to think when you were little I could tolerate you. And Grier, you need to talk to Man-Man about running around here eating up all the snacks and the chicken nuggets. I bought two bags of chicken nuggets and snacks yesterday and by last night they were gone."

"That wasn't me," Man-Man said. "I don't even like chicken nuggets."

"Yes, you do," Toi said.

"Why don't you mind your business?" Man-Man snapped. "This a grown man conversation."

"Then why are you in it?" Toi retorted.

"All right," Ms. Grier said. "Enough. You two know better than to be arguing at the table."

"No, they don't," Cousin Shake said. "Now, my Minnie has finished this food and I want er'body to stand up so we can get our grace on."

We all stood up, held hands, and Cousin Shake began to pray. "Wassup, J to the e to the s to the u to the s?"

What the...

Cousin Shake continued, "What's good wit You and er'-body up there in the Heavens? We wanna thank you for blessing us with another day to get it right. Another day for broke down Lil-Kim a.k.a. Toi to be less hoochie-fied, 'cause I love lil Noah but we don't need another baby up in here. Another day to stop Man-Man from thinking he's a playboy 'cause he grew some hair on his chin and got two hairs on his chest. Another day for Seven to be in the Big Easy but not be the Big Easy. Another day to stop Gymnasium's stank attitude. Another day—"

"All right, Cousin Shake," Ms. Grier said sternly.

"And another day to show their mama that I'm not scared of her. That I raised her, she didn't raise me. And another day to show my Minnie that I love her for more than just her body. I love her for her mind and that body is just extra."

"It sure is," Man-Man said, and then tried to play off what he'd just said by coughing like crazy. I patted him on the back.

"Is it something wrong with you, Man-Man?" Cousin Shake asked.

"Nah, nah, I'm good. Just that visual of Ms. Minnie's body tore me up from the floor up. I'm straight now, though."

"Amir," Ms. Grier said sternly, "Be quiet."

"Yeah," Cousin Shake said, "you better shut 'im down. 'Cause I bet' not catch him side-eyeing Minnie. Now bow your heads and let me finish my prayer."

We complied and Cousin Shake went on. "As I was saying, we just wanna thank You Brother John, I mean Jesus, for putting us on our way and getting these busters ready for school. Let 'em know, Lawd, that the rules have changed. Along with all of my many duties around here I also double as the homework police. Let 'em know none of their lil lazy and crazy friends better not call here after nine. 'Cause if they do, they will be subjected to a Cousin Shake cuss out. So, yeah, I'm 'bout to close this prayer out. And thank Ya for er'thang. The air we breathe and the blood running warm in our veins. And this we pray in my play-cousin Jerry, I mean Jesus' name. Amen."

What kind of...

I looked at Man-Man and he said, "Just let it go. Trust me, eat, and leave it alone."

I took Man-Man's advice and began to eat my breakfast of cheese grits, fried eggs, bacon, and orange juice. "So, Gem are you excited to start school today?" Toi asked.

"No." I stuffed a piece of bacon into my mouth. "I'm cool. It's just school."

"Just school!" Man-Man screeched. "Man, it's more than school, it's a lover boy's playground—and my specialty is turning out all the freshmen."

"I thought you and Pop made up?" I said confused.

"Nah, we always break up on the first day of school. Give me a chance to scout things out and give her something to complain about."

"She needs to dump you and never look back," Toi said.

"She loves me."

"That 'cause she doesn't know you don't have any money. And nobody likes a broke pimp," Toi snapped.

"Amir, you better not be pimpin' anything but those grades," Ms. Grier said.

"Ma," Man-Man said. "I got this." He turned to Toi. "Back up off of G-Bread now. Fall back."

Cousin Shake cut in, "You just better get yourself together, M.C. Alphabet. Now don't make me volunteer as the teacher's aide just to watch you, Man-Man 'cause I'll do it."

"Can you be the teacher's aide at my school, Cousin Shake?" Malik said excited. "Then I don't have to be alone."

"Malik," Miss Grier said. "You won't be alone. You'll make plenty of friends."

"Baby-Tot-Tot," Cousin Shake said. "All the kids gon' like you otherwise they'll have to deal with me!"

Malik laughed. "I really hope the kids are nice."

"Why are you sweatin' that?" I snapped.

"Because I'm scared the kids won't like me," Malik admitted.

"They will like you," I said, hoping Malik would cut the feeling-sorry-for-himself shenanigans. "And you know they will."

"But I hate being the new kid."

"Get. Over. It," I said tight-lipped.

"Don't be so hard on him, Gem," Ms. Grier said. "How about this, Malik. How would you like it if I took you to school this morning? I have a friend whose son is going to be in the same grade as you, and I would love to introduce you two. I have a feeling that you will turn out to be great friends."

"Okay!" Malik's face lit up and I didn't know whether to feel happy that Ms. Grier was being nice or to feel annoyed because Malik needed to get it together.

I decided to nix it. I had my own day to worry about.

"All right," Cousin Shake announced. "Time's up!"

Ms. Minnie cleared the table. "You all have a wonderful day!"

"That's right," Cousin Shake added. "Enjoy your day and just know I love y'all."

Just when I thought he was a monster, he proves that he's human.

"Bye, Ms. Minnie. Bye, Cousin Shake," we all said, leaving the kitchen.

"Malik, where are your sneakers?" Ms. Grier asked as we headed toward the front door.

"Oh, I forgot to put them on." He ran upstairs to his room.

"All right," Toi said. "I have to get Noah to daycare and get to class! Bye."

"Oh, snap," Man-Man said as he patted the side pocket of his jeans. "I must've left my phone upstairs. Hold up for a minute, Gem." He raced up the stairs, and left me and Ms. Grier standing here together.

After a moment of silence Ms. Grier said, "So, Gem, you look really cute this morning."

"Thank you."

"Are you excited?"

"No, I'm going to tenth grade, not kindergarten." I knew I shouldn't have said that, but I couldn't help it. I'd been asked that question twice and both times it reminded me that I was anything but excited. "I'ma go and check on Malik and see what's taking him so long."

Before she could go off I'd run up the stairs and into Malik's room.

"Yo," I said to him. "What's taking you so long?"

"What are you doing in here?" he said in a panic.

"Wondering why you're taking so long. Duh."

"I can't find my sneakers."

I pointed to a corner in his room where sneaker boxes were stacked on top of each other. "Ms. Grier bought you tons of sneakers, wear another pair."

"No, Baby-Tot-Tot has to look sharp, like Cousin Shake said." Malik shook his head. "And I have to wear my Vans on the first day."

I rolled my eyes toward the ceiling. "You gon' make everybody late." I walked around the room, to help him look for the sneakers.

"I don't need your help," Malik snapped at me.

"Boy, please." I waved him off, got on my knees, and looked under the bed.

"I said I don't need your help!" he screamed.

"I already know it's a zoo under here." I dipped my head under the bed. "So don't...yell at me...again!" There was a ton of stuff under this bed, none of which I could really see because under the bed was dark. "You need to clean up!" I grabbed a garbage bag and dragged it from under his bed.

"What is going on up here?" Ms. Grier said walking in. "What's taking you so long? You two need to get going."

"I was trying to help him look for his Vans."

"They are hanging on the shoe rack," she said. "I put them there last night. All you had to do was look behind the door."

Duh!

Ms. Grier grabbed the sneakers as I stood up and dusted my jeans. The bag I'd just dragged from under Malik's bed caught my eye. It was an untied black garbage bag with food and loads of snacks inside...

What the...

I peeped at Malik and he held his head down. I felt like choking him.

I don't believe this. I took my foot and tried to kick the bag back under the bed. It was too bulky to fit back in place easily, and all my foot did was rip it.

"What are you doing, Gem?" Ms. Grier asked. She walked over to where I stood and pointed to the garbage bag.

"Nothing, I was just—"

"About to lie," she completed my sentence. "Now what is that?" She reached for the bag and looked at Malik. "Young man, when I told you to clean up your room yesterday I didn't mean stuff the trash under the bed! I see you and your big brother have a lot in common." She picked up the torn bag and everything in it fell out and splattered across the carpeted floor: cereal, chicken nuggets, fruit snacks, chips, and a box of Capri Sun juice.

Dead...

"What is this?" Ms. Grier asked. The expression on her face let me know that she was not feeling this and she was not feeling us.

On to high school number four.

"Malik, why is there food under your bed?" she asked. "Is this the food Cousin Shake said was missing?"

I looked at Malik and his eyes welled with tears. "I'm sorry," he mumbled. "Gem, tell her I'm sorry."

I wanted to spaz—big time. Malik knew we didn't need to give these fools any reason to trip. And it wasn't like I'd never spoken to him about stealing food before in other foster homes. Actually, I don't even know why he stole the food—maybe it was like he was trying to make up for the times we starved.

Malik had to know this would cause mad trouble...or maybe since the foster parents always blamed the missing food on me and I always took the weight, Malik really didn't know or understand the drama that always went down.

But whatever. All I knew is that this little dude was trippin'. Hard.

"Malik," Ms. Grier said patiently. "Why was there food under your bed?"

He didn't say a word. But I did. "I did it."

She blinked. "What?"

"I did it."

She twisted her full lips. "And why would you steal food?"

I shrugged. "Habit, I guess."

"Habit?"

"Yeah, I mean. My fault."

"Your fault." Ms. Grier arched her brow. "Were you scared you would go hungry, starve, or that the food would disappear?"

I hesitated and then I figured whatever. "Yeah, that's it. I went hungry too many times to count and since all I know is how to survive I was scared to be hungry again. So I started stealing food and hiding it under my bed—"

"It was under Malik's bed," Ms. Grier said.

"Yeah, that's what I meant. Hide it under Malik's bed."

Ms. Grier gave me a half a smile. "You're a wonderful big sister, but a terrible liar. And don't lie to me again. Now, Malik come here."

Malik didn't move.

Ms. Grier repeated herself. "Come. Here."

Tears slid down his cheeks as he slowly walked over to her. "Yes."

She lifted his chin. "Look at me."

He lifted his eyes toward her and before she could say anything he said, "You gon' put us out?"

Ms. Grier paused and then she hugged Malik tightly. "Oh, baby, let me tell you something. As long as you'll have me and my crazy family this is your home."

"Really?" he said anxiously. "So you're not mad at me."

"No," she said. "I just want you to understand that you don't need to steal food because whatever we have here is yours. It's not going anywhere. It won't disappear, and I will never let you starve." She lifted her eyes and looked at me. "Ever," she said. "And I mean it."

And I knew she meant it, I just didn't want to deal with any mushy, emotional or heavy stuff right now. I just wanted—for once—to have a regular day. No worries. No aggravation. No baggage.

"Yo, Gem!" Man-Man yelled up the stairs. "Let's go! I need to get to school a few minutes early to stroll around the grounds."

Saved.

"Let's roll!" he yelled again.

Gladly.

I looked at Ms. Grier and said, "I gotta go."

"And we both know you're in no rush." Ms. Grier smiled at me and surprisingly I smiled back; mostly because I couldn't help it. "Have a good day," she said.

"You too," I said as I raced out of the room. I couldn't get out of there fast enough and just as I headed toward the stairs I heard Malik say, "I love you, Ms. Grier!"

11

"Let me school you on Brick City High politics," Man-Man said as wide and purple lace panties dangled from the rearview mirror of his black '01 Civic Hatchback. The panties swayed like a ribbon in the morning breeze. I was disgusted. Lip turned up and face frowned disgusted.

"What's wrong with you?" Man-Man said as we drove up the street. "Ms. Minnie's fried eggs tearing up your stomach?"

"The only thing tearing up my stomach are those wide behind lace panties dangling from your mirror. Are those clean?"

He gleamed. "First of all, don't disrespect the trophy. And yeah, they're clean 'cause I washed 'em. And they're not wide, they're just right."

"For who?"

"My boos. Big girls. I love 'em. I can't stand no skinny chicks." Man-Man frowned like he had something bitter in his mouth.

"And why not? What skinny girls ever do to you?"

"They just don't feel right. Whenever I tried to hug one I felt like I was being attacked by a paper cut. Nah, I like my honeys the same way I like my chicken: plump, big thighs. Nice and thick. Juicy. But don't get it confused, although I like big girls I have a limit. I like a hungry man's dinner, not a buffet. Feel me?"

How about no... "So those panties belong to some random chick. How nasty."

"You buggin'. I bought those panties out of Dollar Tree. They belong to me."

"You own a pair of lace panties and I'm buggin'? Yeah, okay." I side-eyed him.

"You need to get your mind right. 'Cause if you broadened your horizons you'd understand that those panties keep me focused."

"Focused?" I couldn't help but laugh. "On what? Big booties?"

"There you go, mind all in the gutter. Ma raised me to be a respectable young man. I like girls for the veins in their brains."

"What?"

"You know what I mean."

"Yeah, I know exactly what you mean."

He continued, "So I bought the panties because when I meet my plus-sized queen and I ask her to be my girl, I'ma give her the lace panties to wear."

"Boom," I said sarcastically and snapped my fingers. "It'll be like a ring."

"Pow, there it is," Man-Man said. "Like a drop down crown. And if ya girl Pop gets herself together maybe she'll get her upgrade on, be back in wifey status, and these panties just might be in her future. Dig?"

"How rewarding. I'm sure she'll love that." *Not.*

"You know my motto: go big or shut da hell up."

"Yeah, those big panties prove that."

"And there it is. Now let's get back to politickin'."

"Let's."

"So check it: at Brick City High I run the Player's Club."

"Why am I not surprised?"

"'Cause you know how I do it. And peep this—I'm not only a client, I'm the Player president." He popped his invisible collar.

O...M...G...straight clownin'... And while Man-Man tripped off of his own swag and laid down his laws of the land, my mind drifted to thoughts of Ny'eem. I was feeling him like crazy...I just didn't know what to say to him, which is why I had yet to call him back. He'd called me two days in a row. Left messages on my cell phone and not once did I dial his number. I just didn't know what to say to him.

"Yeah, hello..." was my failed attempt to ac out our conversation. Even to myself I sounded stupid so I knew he would think I was dumb.

I looked toward Man-Man, who was s running his mouth about his favorite subject, him ...Yeah, my Player's Club presidency will go down history because it's only one of me. And any more hat would be disastrous."

Fa' real though. "Man-Man derstand there are no

He continued, "People ead—"

clones of Man-Man. I me

I snapped my fingers and waved my hands for attention. "Excuse me, can you get off of planet Myself and come back to Earth with everyone else? I need to ask you something."

Man-Man looked at me like I was crazy. "That was hella rude."

"Would you listen to me? I want to ask you something."

"What?" he said as we stopped at the light. "Wassup?"

"I want you to be serious, okay?"

"I'm always serious." The light turned green and he took off. "What you think I be playin'? Nah, what you see is straight up G. See, I be telling these girls that I'ma real cat. Never been phony—"

"This is so not about you."

He looked taken aback. "Then what is this about?"

"Me." I pointed to my chest. "Gem. So, can the conversation focus on me for five minutes?" I held my hand up.

"Yo, you can calm down. What's all the attitude about?"

"Are you going to let me get a word in?"

"Go 'head."

I swallowed and don't ask me why I was nervous, but I was. And don't ask me why I wanted Man-Man's opinion, but I did. I huffed. Let out a strong string of air and said this quickly. "Doboyslikegirlslikeme?"

"I got a D in Spanish, so I'ma need you to say that again but hold up me in English. And not honors English either. 101."

"Do. Boys. Lik Man-Man hesitals. Like. Me?"

his head. "I knew th Umm…" He paused and shook

I smirked and look ld happen."

what?"   m, completely put off. "Knew

"I knew that my swagaliciousness would cause you to take side glances at me."

"Say that again."

"But check it, I know I'm irresistible, tantalizing, and desirable. But the day you came to live with us, Ma laid down the law that you were family. Period. Dot. Dot. Dot. And the moment she declared you were my sister you became like...how do I say this without hurting your feelings?" He snapped his fingers. "Nasty looking to me. Real stank."

"Nasty looking and real stank?" *Did he just say nasty looking and real stank?*

"Don't trip. I mean you're cute and all but, we can't go there. Besides, I think it's illegal and I can't do jail. I stole a CD out of Walmart once, Ma made me do Scared Straight and yo, that whole deal messed...me...up. And ever since then I break out into nigh sweats and start screaming, 'I don't wanna wash your drawls, Pookie!' "

Why did I even bother? "Look," I said. "I'm not looking at you sideways, front ways, from the back, or any other kind of way, actually I don't even understand why all these girls be sweatin' you, fa' real."

"Was that a diss?"

"Anyway, all I wanna know is if you think that boys, *and not you*, like girls like me?"

Man-Man looked me over, from head to stiletto, and back again. "I think," he tapped his temple, "that a cat could think you looked a'ight. You okay."

"A'ight? Okay? That's it?"

"Yeah, that's it. I mean if you're looking for something to boost your self-esteem you gon' have to watch the *Bad Girls Club* or *Jersey Shore*, 'cause I don't do all of that."

"Oh...my...God..."

"What's the problem? I mean, you good. I guess. And why you asking me that anyway?"

" 'Cause." I blushed. "I kind of like somebody."

"Who?" he pressed.

"One of your boys."

"Oh, hell nawl," he pounded against the steering wheel. "You messing up the constitution. It's a violation for little sisters and their brother's boys to be kickin' it."

"No it's not."

He sighed. "Who is it?"

"It's umm—"

"Oh hold up. Hold. Up. Yo, that night of the party when I couldn't find you and I stepped outside and you were talking to Ny'eem, were y'all talking, like 'hey wassup?' or were y'all kicking it like 'Hey. Wassup?' "

I paused, especially since I wanted to say, "We did more than kick it—actually his swag and his kisses took me hostage and that's why I'm so torn on whether I need to run away or stand and deal with the flurries running through my belly." But I decided to keep it simple. "We were kicking it."

"I knew it. Y'all exchanged numbers?"

"Yeah, he gave me his number."

Man-Man shook his head. "You talk to him?"

"No."

"Good, don't. I don't want you talking to my boys." He made a left into the school's parking lot.

"Are you serious?"

He shook his head again. "I see I'ma have to watch you. But whatever, Ny'eem is cool, so I guess it'll be a'ight if y'all kicked it for a minute. You called him?"

"No. I didn't know what to say to him."

"Just let it flow. Ny'eem is a cool dude. And if he wasn't feeling you he wouldn't have even kicked it to you. So he must like you."

"Really?" I couldn't stop smiling.

"Close your mouth. And yeah, really. If Ny'eem gave you his number then he's diggin' you."

"Maybe I'll just talk to him when I see him this morning."

"You won't. He doesn't go to school here, he lives on the block but he goes to a private school. They recruited him to play ball."

"Word?"

"Yup. And you know they tried to recruit me, too."

"Really?"

"Yeah, I tried out to be a center and they gon' recruit me to be the mascot. What I look like running around with a hot-and-played bear costume on?"

All I could do was laugh. Actually, I laughed so hard I cried.

"I don't find that funny," Man-Man said. "I'm a little sensitive about that."

"Oh, okay. I'm sorry." I did my best to stop giggling. "My fault."

"Anyway," Man-Man said quickly changing the subject, "while Ny'eem's over at his school running thangs I'm here in Brick City High handling my lane—the mac game." He took the key from the ignition. "So what you gon' do? You gon' call him or what?"

"I—"

"Excuse me, Gem," Man-Man cut me off as a group of girls walked past the car. "Hold that thought for a few hours." He got out of the car, dipped across the lot, and walked over to the group of girls who quickly enveloped him. No good-bye. No see you later. Nothing. Just a cloud of dust left behind.

I eased out the car and leaned against the door. I turned my head and looked around the school's parking lot. It was a sea of color, varying fashion, and teens of all shapes and sizes. There were cackles of laughter, buzzing conversations filled the air, and teachers patrolled the parking lot.

I walked over to the school—an enormous, three-story, beige brick building—and walked in through the glass door. There were pockets of cliques everywhere, which caused me to be hesitant once I stood at the top of the hallway.

I hated starting all over again.

New friends.

New teachers.

Ugh, I was so not beat for this.

12

My stilettos clapped against the tile floor as I put one four-inch heel in front of the other, and did my all to ease to my locker. My intention was to keep a low profile and peep things out. Find out who was real, who was phony, and whose mouth was always in somebody's business. This way I'd know when to keep my distance. It's not that I was an angel. I mean, sometimes I liked to watch ish unfold—a little—I just didn't like drama sneaking up on me. I preferred a warning.

Feel me?

Exactly. So I decided to creep to my locker while nobody noticed me.

"Geeeeeem!" Pop shrieked my name like a bolt of lightning. Everyone turned and looked dead in my face.

So much for incognito...

Pop carried on. "Over here, girl! Over here!" She blew a pink bubble and popped it while placing one hand on her hip and the other in the air. "That's my girl right there!"

she broadcasted to the crowd in the hallway. "Yup, that's right! My best-bestie in the whole world. Okay!" She paused, took a breath, and continued, "Let me tell y'all something, you may think these lil freaks, and frenemies, and so called homies are your friends, but none of them are like this chick right here. 'Cause this chick is totally different. She knows the meaning of having her girl's back fa' sho." Pop parked her hips one way and her neck another. "Now don't hate, appreciate and get ya clap on for my homegirl, Gem!"

And as if that speech itself wasn't embarrassing enough some folks really clapped their hands. I didn't know if they were being anti-hatin', sarcastic, or if Pop had enough popularity and pull to make me a rock star. But whatever it was I had to live up to my rep at the moment so I kicked things up to a red carpet notch and hit 'em with a Beyoncé strut down the runway.

I popped my hips from left to right, posed, turned, posed, and sauntered toward my friend, who I knew if nobody else in the world had my back, she did—no matter how long we'd been apart. We both giggled at my performance as we embraced.

"I missed you so much," Pop squealed and squeezed me. "I'm so glad we go to the same school!"

"Me too," I said.

"Girl," Pop took a step back and snapped her fingers the way she always did when she was either mad or excited. "Boo-boo, this year..." Snap, snap. "Is 'bout. To. Be. Fiyah!"

"And there it is."

"And just so you know, I wanted to call you this morn-

ing, so that we could've met in the parking lot somewhere. But just as I went to text G and tell him to have you
call me I got an e-mail alert that read, *'G-Bread has
changed his relationship status.'* So I peeped out his
Facebook page and don't you know he changed his status
from 'Happily kicking it,' to 'It's complicated.' Can you believe that? 'Cause I couldn't believe that! It's the first day
of school and now I'ma complication? Me? And you know
I'm drama free. Always. So there is nothing complicated
about me." Snap. Snap. Deep breath.

I didn't know what amazed me more: that she said all
of that in one breath or that she thought Man-Man's Facebook status was that deep. Heck, he's not even that deep,
and besides, I didn't really wanna talk about him. "Pop,
now you know you're too cute to be sweatin' anybody. Let
him sweat you."

"Oh girl, I know. I'm ca'yute. No doubt." Snap. Snap.
Sucked teeth. "Forget him. And besides, I did him one better and changed my status to single. Boom. *And* I blocked
him *and* unfollowed him on Twitter. If he can say that I'm
a complication then I can ban him from my page and stop
following his tweets around."

Oh…my…God…

"But did he mention me this morning?" she spat out as
if she couldn't keep the question bottled up a moment
longer.

Pause. Ummm… "Yeah."

"What he say, girl?" Her eyes burst with excitement.
"Was he crying and mad, 'cause I'm single now or was he
spittin' fire 'cause I blocked him? Or was he really beat because I made his number of Twitter followers drop down."

"I'm not sure about any of that. But I know he said something about you being wifey." *I can't believe I'm in the middle of this, again.*

"I knew it." Snap. Snap. Pop blew a pink bubble and popped it. "But it's cool, 'cause I'ma make him wait it out at least four days, four hours, four and a half minutes, and a few seconds before I even think about taking him back. Hmph, I need some time to do me. And get my mind together. 'Cause obviously G got me twisted. "

Ummm hmmm....

"Anywho girl," Pop said, "enough of him. Let me tell you I was so worried that you wouldn't know what door to come in. God forbid you got mixed up with the freaky freshmen." She fanned her face. "You didn't get mixed up with those creatures did you?"

"Creatures—?"

"Creatures, honey. Lil nasty eighth graders who just graduated elementary school. And the boys are the worst. Those lines they lay on you, oh my. I'm telling you they will make you understand why folks need the Holy Ghost. Now did you run into any of them this morning?"

"No."

"Good. 'Cause the way you were standing here like a frozen Pop-Tart I was concerned."

All I could do was laugh.

"Now let me look at you." Pop took a step back and waved her index finger over me like a wand. "Check, check."

"Check, check what?" I twisted my lip in confusion.

"Check, check you look cute," she said and snapped her fingers.

"Rich Girl fly."

"And you know this. That's why I can't wait 'til we get up on the court together and kill 'em!" She made an invisible three-point play. "Swoosh! The crowd goes wild and the opposing team goes down!"

We cracked up laughing at least until Kamani slammed the door to her locker and said, "Don't get carried away. 'Cause first of all to be a true Rich Girl—"

"Means you're a part of the b-ball team," Janay said to us as she walked over and completed Kamani's sentence.

"And last I checked," Kamani continued, "you were the new chick on the block."

"Who was not a part of the team," Janay said.

Pop interjected, "Are you two even serious with this right now?"

"I know that's your girl and all Pop," Kamani said. "But rules are rules and she can't be a Rich Girl just because she knows you." She looked me over. "And that's just how it is. I mean I heard you could ball and all—"

"The best who ever did it," I said with one hundred percent confidence.

"But you're not on the team. Now, tryouts are next week, which all adds up to this—you're getting a little ahead of yourself."

I couldn't believe this chick. Trust, if I were on the street I would've molly-whopped this heifer by now. Dragged her over the concrete. "You seem confused, boo, because I'm the one who started the whole Rich Girl crew—" I said.

"You didn't start nothing over here—!" Kamani spazzed.

"Yes, she did," Pop said. "I shared the name with y'all,

because we were a nameless clique. But the Rich Girlz started when Gem and I were twelve and Gem suggested it. We had a constitution and the whole nine. Matter fact Gem is the one who gave us our sole rule, 'No Boyz allowed to come between our crew.' She's the one—"

"Who disappeared and you haven't seen her in four years," Kamani snapped. "Now it's cool and cute if she's who truly named the clique, but it's been upgraded since she was last in it. And now you have to be a Brick City High baller to be a part of it. And since I'm the captain of the basketball team she has to come through me. Period. And right now I'm not sure how I'm feeling."

"You know what," I said disgusted. "This is just too much. Like, fa' real-fa' real, it's not even that deep for me. My life is so much more than this silliness. So check it, the last thing on my mind is rolling with a group of chicks. And for the record I don't eff with basketball anymore 'cause if I did you'd be benched, Captain."

Kamani sucked her teeth and flicked her hand. "Girl, please."

"Yeah, and that's just how you'd spend your time: begging me." I turned to Pop. "You're my girl and all, but silly chicks and their tricks are for kids."

"Gem, just chill," Pop said and then turned to Kamani. "You need to fall back, Kamani. It's the first day of school and nobody came here for fever."

"Don't try and blame me. I wasn't trying to start anything," Kamani said. "I was just making a statement and Gem got all twisted about it."

"Girl, bye. I don't have to deal with you." Then as if on cue the bell rang, and mobs of teens scattered toward their homerooms.

"I guess we'll get up," Janay said, as she turned to follow behind Kamani who'd walked away and into our
homeroom.

"Yeah, I guess we'll get up," Pop said somberly, like she
was lost. And I guess in a way she was lost because I didn't
know what to say. I expected my day to go one way but it
had totally flipped the script—so clearly, I wasn't in
charge.

My homeroom teacher stood in the doorway and said,
"You ladies have two minutes to make it in here or you'll
have to go to the guidance counselor's office and get a late
pass."

Pop and I didn't say anything; we just walked into the
classroom and an awkward silence followed behind us. I
took my seat and as Pop sat next to me, she turned toward
the back of the room and looked at Janay and Kamani.
There was an empty desk between them, I guess that's
where Pop would've sat if I wasn't here. "You don't have
to sit here if you don't want to," I said. The last thing I
wanted was for her to feel obligated to me. "Psst, please.
I'm good."

"If I wanted to move I would," Pop said.

I didn't say anything more. The awkward silence resumed and consumed my entire time in homeroom. I
guess that's why I was so surprised and caught off guard
when the bell rang again signaling that class had ended.
Everybody rushed out of the room and Pop and I lagged
behind. Once we stood in the hallway I turned to her and
said, "Look, you don't have to feel obligated to hang with
me. You got your b-ball crew and obviously they're not
feeling me and I'm def not feeling them. So you know . . .

I'm okay with us being reduced to just being cool. Nothing more. Nothing less."

"Oh, really?" Pop's eyes looked as if they were turning red, but she shook it off and looked at me as if I'd lost my mind.

I continued, "I'm just saying, it's not written anywhere that we have to be homegirls."

"We don't have to anything actually," she snapped.

I felt like she'd taken her hand and slapped me, so I said, "It's not like we were much anyway, your grandmother died and after the funeral your family hurried to get rid of me. None of y'all ever looked for me or my brother. So, it's whatever. 'Cause whether you continue to be my bestie or not won't change a thing for me."

Pop hesitated and then she said, "Why you trippin' again?" And she must've been straight serious, 'cause not once did she snap her fingers or twist her neck. "Yeah, Janay and Kamani are my girls and all but neither one of them are my besties. So you can just cut the extra."

"I'm not being extra."

"Yeah right, if you're not being extra then why would you say you don't eff with ball anymore?"

And where did that come from? "What? Why are you even on that?"

"'Cause I wanna know what's really good with that? Like, that just seems to be some bull dot com, dot org, dot ridiculous."

"What's it to you? Ball just ain't for me anymore. Now skip it."

"You're lyin'. You love ball more than anybody I know—"

"Well maybe you don't know me!" I yelled and my voice

boomed through the hallway, causing some of the students to look our way.

"I know you better than you know yourself!" Pop snapped. "And I know you're not keepin' it real with me. And whatever you're running from doesn't have a thing to do with ball or me for that matter. It has to do with you. So I don't know why you're taking it out on us! What you need to do is deal with yourself and stop thinking that everybody is out to get you—!"

"Don't tell me what I need to do! And why you sweatin' me so hard about basketball? What, does your team suck? Did your nice little college coach daddy tell you to step it up a notch so you can be recruited? Are you trying to be my friend or are you trying to get your team to win!"

"You can't even be serious!"

"Dead serious!" I snapped. "As a matter of fact I'm cool on you and this bull!"

"Gem—!"

"Step off!" I said, and stormed down the hall, frustrated, pissed, and angry. I was sooooo over the nonsense. As a matter of fact I was over this day! And instead of hooking a left to math class, I clicked my heels down the tile runway—the same one I'd sauntered down an hour ago—and walked right out the exit door.

I had to blow this place or it was gon' be a situation. Trust. 'Cause the next person who came at me crazy was gon' catch it. Believe dat. So I walked to the corner bus stop and hopped on the first thing that came my way.

13

For two hours I rode the city bus from one end of Newark to the other and I was heated the whole ride. I just wanted to scream, or punch something, or just...I don't know...all I knew is that I wanted to lose it on somebody somewhere for something. I just didn't know who, what, or why...I just did.

And to keep it all the way one hundred, if I could ride this bus to the end of the Earth I would...but with five dollars in my pocket I knew I didn't have enough money to get there. And the last time I tried to jet with five dollars...let's just say it was a problem.

Outside of the bus's aged plexiglass window the city passed by in snapshots of traffic, mobs of people, children playing in the park, and memories. Memories of my mother and how much we begged her to stay home because we believed that would magically make her clean. But it didn't, because she always chose the streets...always...

I hadn't seen her in almost two years and I wondered how she was. Did she think about me...or Malik...? About us being a family? Or was out of sight truly out of mind? As the bus continued to ride up Springfield Avenue I felt an urge to find my mother, and ask her if she planned on picking us up from hell or were we supposed to live there...

I pressed the buzzer. "Next stop, please," I yelled to the driver. He pulled up to the littered curb and I stepped off. I walked a little ways down Springfield Avenue until I got to 21st Street. Once I was on 21st Street I walked past a few abandoned buildings until I got to the one my mother lived in. It was a two family shack with boarded up windows, glass everywhere, graffiti all over it, and no front door. There was a river of trash that flowed from the hallway and down the stairs.

It felt weird being here, knowing that once upon a time this block and this house was lit up with life and now it was dead—the people included. And I knew from the moment my heels splashed in a puddle of piss I had no business being here. But this was where my mother was and I needed to see her.

She was easy to spot, too. She sat on the crowded stoop with her legs crossed and her eyes staring off into the distance. She wore the same dingy jeans that she had on the last time we saw each other.

The oversized green T-shirt she had on hung off one shoulder and revealed her sunken collarbone.

Seeing my mother like this was like having an out of body experience. Like was this really my mother? Really? So I was really the kid of a chicken head...I hated that.

I started to walk, scratch that, I started to run back

down the street, but quickly changed my mind. I was already here and I needed to deal with this . . . with her.

I walked closer to the stoop and stared at my mother. I could tell by the way she squinted that she didn't recognize me.

"Ma," I called out to her and everybody on the stoop looked toward me.

My mother squinted. Hesitated. But still no recognition.

"Ma, it's me. Gem." I did my all to smile but the corners of my lips barely lifted.

My mother pulled a cigarette from her jeans pocket and lit it. She took a long pull, titled her head toward the heavens, and let out a long string of smoke. Afterward she looked back to me and narrowed her eyes. "What is you doin' here?" was her version of hello.

I paused, caught off guard. I took a step back and then two steps forward. "I umm . . . wanted to talk to you."

She sucked her teeth and shook her head. "'Bout what?" She took a puff and snorted. "I ain't got no money, matter fact I need you to give me some money."

"Ain't that right," signified one of the women who sat next to my mother. "Sho' need some money."

"Ma," I said, not knowing what else to say. "I don't have any money."

"Ain't you grown?"

"Ma." I swallowed. "I'm just sixteen."

"That's grown. Grown enough to go out there and make some money. Hmph." She pointed to a greasy old man, who'd been watching me ever since I'd crossed the street. "Mr. John pay real good. And you pretty, too. Remind me of myself when I was your age." She turned to a woman sitting next to her. "Ain't she pretty? That's why I named her Gem because she reminded me of a chocolate diamond. Now anybody that pretty," she turned back to me, "should never have to walk the street with no money. And their mama shouldn't be broke either."

Silence.

"So where you staying?" she snorted. "Look like you staying some place nice?"

"It's okay." I shrugged.

"Well, you know they ain't yo family, right?"

"Do I have a family? Last I checked I was doing this alone." I knew I shouldn't have said that, but I couldn't help it. I couldn't.

My mother stood up. "Don't make me come over there and smack the crazy outta you."

Whatever.

"So you better get it straight," she said. "I'm ya mama."

"So does that mean you're going to get yourself to-gether or is this it?"

My mother squinted, placed both hands on her hips and her burning cigarette dangled loosely from her mouth. "Who in the hell is you talking to? You don't talk to me like that!"

"I'm just askin'." I shrugged again. "I mean, it's no big deal. I've been doin' it this long."

"Look, I did my best!"

"Really?"

"Hell, yeah I did. So don't be trying to blame me for a damn thing! I did all I could to get y'all back home with me, but that social worker told me that I couldn't."

I twisted my lips. "And why would she tell you that?"

"Ask her. She got that answer. 'Cause I did my part. And

who you really need to be questionin' is your sister Kera with her fast behind. Lying and saying that I had men in my house touching her so I could buy crack."

"She said that because that's what you did! So it's not her fault. It's your fault 'cause now she's in the nut house half crazy and can't think straight. Saying people are calling her names and she's the only one that can hear them!"

"Your sister lied, that's why she's crazy as hell! Now I don't know what you came here for, but I can't help you. I'm barely making it myself. So you better take your fresh behind back where you came from, 'cause I ain't got nothin' for you."

Although I stood and faced her with my mouth twisted and a don't care attitude on my face, inside I was stoned. Paralyzed. Gut punched. Goose bumps ran down my back as I realized that I had the answer I'd been looking for— my mother planned on leaving us in hell. She never planned on saving us.

Ever...

I sniffed. Fought back tears and rocked my game face. "It's really not that serious. And you sure don't have to worry about me coming around here ever again. 'Cause I got this and me and my brother gon' be good without you!"

"Later," my mother said unimpressed.

I swallowed. This was crazy. Absolutely crazy. Problem was if I knew this was crazy then why did it make me feel soooo messed up, like I was spinning out of control.

I did all I could to shake it off as I walked back to the bus stop and my mother disappeared into the distance behind me.

* * *

"I need to hollah at you for a minute," Pop said with a serious attitude as she folded her arms across her breasts and tapped her foot.

I'd just stepped off the bus and had crossed the street when I spotted Pop sitting on the porch, obviously waiting for me.

I turned to her and just as I went to tell her that I wasn't in the mood she said, "I'm not leaving until I say what I have to say. So we gon' either do this out here or do this in your room. But either way you will hear me out today. Right now."

"Whatever," I said as I walked into the house and she followed me. I cut through the living room, which was empty. Thank God, because I didn't have to deal with a million questions about where I'd been and why I'd cut school.

I walked up the stairs to my room. Pop shut the door behind me and instantly started going in, "That lil gabba-gabba-bustin' off at me you did in school, when I didn't even do anything to you, I didn't appreciate. Now I don't know what your problem is, but we need to deal with it!"

I shook my head and fought back the tears I felt beating against the back of my eyes like drums. A big part of me wanted to scream on Pop and tell her to just beat it, but I couldn't. Tears had already started down my cheeks and I knew there was no way she would leave now. No matter what I said.

"Gem," Pop said in a panic as she sat on the bed next to me. "What's wrong? Tell me."

Silence. I did all I could to suck back my tears, but they

wouldn't stop coming and instead it felt like behind my face a dam had broken.

Pop wiped my eyes with the back of her thumbs. "You gotta stop trying to be so tough all the time. You can't do everything alone. Let somebody in. Yo, we're best friends and after all these years we've found each other. We're like family again. Don't shut me out. What's up? Tell me. 'Cause that's what besties are for."

Just tell her... ugg... just say it. "I've been soooo pissed off."

"Why?"

"'Cause... all of these years I really thought that one day my mother was gon' get herself together."

"Well maybe she will. You never know—"

"Pop," I said, wiping my eyes. "It's not gon' happen."

"How do you know that?"

"'Cause I went to see her when I left school."

"And?"

"*And* she didn't even know who I was. And once she found out, she didn't even care. It didn't even matter to her. She didn't ask me how I was, how my brother was, nothing. Do you know what she asked me for?"

"What?"

"Money." Pop gave a low gasp as I continued. "And when I told her I didn't have any, she told me I was too pretty not to have any money. So she pointed to this dirty old man on the street and told me to go and see him 'cause he paid well."

"What?"

"She was trying to sell me." Tears raced from my eyes. "My mother is nothing. And if my mother is nothing then I have to be less than that."

"Gem…" Pop paused and then hugged me. I cried until all I could see was a faded blur.

Don't look now, but I've perfected pathetic. After a few minutes of giving in to feeling sorry for myself I held my head up from Pop's shoulder and to my surprise we were both wiping tears. "Now look." She fanned her face. "You gon' have to chill with these tears 'cause I didn't wear my waterproof mascara and G is downstairs. I can't be looking all black-blue and crazy."

Leave it to Pop.

"Now listen," she continued as she reached for my hand and held it between hers. "You gon' ruin yo insides by keeping all this mess, and anger, and ra-ra in there. You can't keep everything all bottled up. It's not good for your system to be walking around on ten all day, ready to get it crunked at any moment. That's the kind of stuff that makes your make-up look crazy and your ballin' all busted. You already know peeps be lookin' at girls who play sports extra-sideways, waiting to see if we gon' spin around and bust out into a double-breasted suit and gaiters. Okay."

"Pop, this is soooo not about ball."

"I know that. I'm just making a point that we are way too cute for tears. And you're my girl, Gem, so if something hurts you then I'm ready to jump in two fist swingin'. Dig? But we can't beat up ya mama because that will not make her change."

"We could sneak her one good time." I chuckled as tears continued to roll down my cheeks.

Pop laughed and wiped my face with the back of her right hand. "Look, your mother is who she is, but one thing she isn't is you. So if you think that, you need to drop it."

"But that's my mother and I feel like when people see me, they see a foster kid with no family and a mother strung out in the streets."

"No they don't, Gem. They see you. Period. But you have to make up your mind what side of you that you want people to see and get to know. Do you want them to know the side of you that's ready to slap folks for saying hello? Or the side of you who I know that's fun to kick it with?"

"I don't want people hating me."

"Then you need to chill and act sixteen and not like that miserable sixty-year-old lady who lives on my street. 'Cause, newsflash, just 'cause she's old doesn't mean anybody likes her. I can't stand her. And in order for her to be a nasty-face-frowned-Polident problem at sixty, means she was giving people the business at sixteen. Feel me?"

"Yeah, I feel you." I shook my head. "But Pop, you have to understand that being sixteen to me—means moving from place to place, having to fight for everything. Having nobody but me and wondering if the people I live with will like me from one day to the next. Or will I be waking up one morning with them telling me it's time to roll."

"Dang, girl. That ain't being sixteen, that's a hot mess."

"Exactly. My life."

"Look, you got it twisted. Maybe that was your life before you came here, but these people are different. And I'm not just saying that because I need you to become my sister-in-law and keep an eye on G for me. I mean, I need that, too, but still. I'm saying this because when I told G that you left school and he didn't know where you were, he looked so worried. And he was so sensitive at that moment that we almost got back together and everything right then, but then I remembered what he did and put him on pause. And after he begged me to reconsider and I didn't, do you know what he told me?"

"What?"

"That he loved having you as his little sister. And he loved Malik, too. He said his mother and stepfather wanted to be here for you, but that you had so much attitude that you couldn't even see it. G said the day that Cousin Shake dragged you down the stairs and tossed you into the kitchen that he knew you were in like Flynn. So I'm telling you pay attention, 'cause they love you. Just chill and ride the wave. Stop thinking about tomorrow, 'cause at sixteen all I think about is today. Tomorrow is a whole other problem. Feel me?"

"I guess," I nodded. "A little."

"You need to feel me all the way, 'cause all you need to be thinking about is boo-lovin' and ballin."

I chuckled. "That's what's most important?"

"Fa'sho. Now stop buggin' and just roll wit it."

"Is it really that easy?"

"It's as easy as Janay after a football game."

Pop and I cracked up laughing. We laughed so hard that we fell back on my bed in tears—happy tears. And I thought, *maybe...maybe...Pop was right.*

Or maybe she was wrong...which one I really didn't know. All I knew is that me being upset and uptight all the time didn't do anything more than work people's nerves and cause me to stay steppin' to folks.

I was tired of that.

And I was tired of a bunch of thoughts about my mother, my life, and where I was going to lay my head at night crowding my mind all the time. I just wanted to think about silly and simple, like boos, and parties, and clothes, and shoes, and Twitter, and Facebook, and make-up, and maybe ballin'. Things that meant nothing, but meant everything all at the same time. I didn't want to worry another day—about being kicked out of another foster home. Like Pop said I just wanted to be sixteen—her version of sixteen. "Just boys and ballin', huh," I said.

"Yep, that's it."

"So maybe I should chill, a little bit."

"You need to chill a whole lot," she smiled.

"So maybe you're right."

"Of course I'm right. My cuteness allows me to know these things. So just trust your bestie, okay?"

I paused. I felt second thoughts creeping up on me, but I shook them off, because I felt like...like I had to do something different, at least I had to try it. "A'ight. I'm game."

"All right now!" Pop hugged me tightly. "We 'bout to make it pop, boo-boo!" She hopped up off the bed. " 'Bout to do it, whaaaat!"

I fell out laughing.

"And from this moment on, all that other stuff, that ain't even relevant," she said. "You know what's relevant?"

"What?"

"This is." She walked over to my radio and turned the volume up. " 'Cause this 'Cupid Shuffle' throwback. Is. My. Jam!"

"Pop, that song is fifty years old."

"I don't care! 'Cause this is my song!" She kicked her legs and broke out into the full fledge Cupid Shuffle.

Pop was so into it there was no way I could sit here and watch her kill the dance by herself. Nah, we both had to put it to sleep. So, I hopped up and together we broke it down. "*Now walk it by yourself…*" we chanted.

This was the perfect ending to the worst day ever; and just when the song changed and we were set to break down the Ole' folk, Man-Man swung my door open—and no, he didn't knock—he just stepped inside, stroked his goatee and said, "So this is how we doin' it? Huh? What part of the game is this? The remix?"

"What are you talking about?" I looked at him strangely.

"Here I been downstairs, repenting and praying to God to just make me a preacher so that Mommy and Khalil didn't kill me, 'cause I let you jump off a bridge."

"I didn't jump off a bridge." I twisted my lips.

"How was I 'spose to know that? All I knew is that you cut school right after homeroom. Like you had a problem that school took up most of your day or somethin'."

"That wasn't it—"

"I don't care what it was. All I know is that I was worried about you and I don't do wrinkles in my forehead."

"Awwl, you were worried about me." I held my arms out and walked toward him to give him a hug.

"Back up," Man-Man said as I wrapped my arms around him and kissed him on the cheek. "Back-up," he repeated, breaking up our hug. "We ain't 'bout to hug this out. I've been struggling to hide out from the homework police. Do you know how hard it is to hide from them? And based on my grades last year, I'm a wanted man right now. I'm hot and they all on my trail."

"Well—"

"Well nothin'. 'Cause I don't believe that all this time you been upstairs throwin' back a throwback and poppin' it to the floor? Well, G-Bread got a lil bit of a problem with that, homie."

"My fault," I said, genuinely feeling bad.

Man-Man never acknowledged my apology; he just turned and started in on Pop. "And yo, this how we droppin' it, Pop?"

"Yop." She smacked her lips and popped her hips. "And I don't have a hug for you, 'cause yop this how we droppin' it, fa'sho. Boom! All on the ground and splattered around."

What the...

"So what you sayin', Pop?" Man-Man walked closer to her. "That you don't love me anymore? That we're over for good?"

Pop smacked her lips. "I didn't say that. Don't be putting words in my mouth."

"So then wassup?" Man-Man said. "Just call it what it is then, 'cause I wanna get back together again, now. Right now. Being without you has killed me."

"Really?" she whined, sweetly. "Being without me has you dead now, G?"

He placed his hands over his eyes like a sun-visor. "I'm so dead, I think I see Moses."

"Awwl." She cupped his face between her palms. "Word?"

"Word." He nodded. "I'm straight trippin' without you."

"Dang, boo." She stroked his face and then took a step back. "Thing is, you gon' have to trip for at least three more days, fifteen hours, twenty-five minutes, and a few seconds, 'cause I'm not feelin' nor appreciatin' what you did." She placed her hands on her hips.

NO BOYZ ALLOWED 107

"What?" Man-Man said shocked. "So we're not getting back together today? Right now, at this moment?"

"Hell to the fourth power of no." She batted her lashes. "You've got Cameron "Popcorn" Hunter messed up. Like I told you earlier today, I didn't like what you did. And you gon' pay for that. How you just gon' change your status to *'It's Complicated'*? You gon' play me, G? Awl hell nawl!"

"Baby, I love you."

"Well, I don't know what to tell you. 'Cause I have standards. Now what you can do is check my Facebook status in three more days, fifteen hours, twenty-five minutes, and a few seconds, and if it reads *'Booed Up'* then we're back together again." Pop swung around and looked at me. "Remember what I told you, Poo."

"I will," I said.

"Pop—" Man-Man called her but she ignored him and instead said to me, "See you tomorrow, meet you at my locker."

"Bye, Pop."

"Bye."

"Pop," Man-Man said, still getting his royal beg on. "Don't do this, Pop. Let me hollah at you for a minute."

Pop clicked her heels out of the room and Man-Man followed behind her. "Don't be like that, Pop," he said as they walked down the stairs. "Pop!" he called her as the front door slammed.

All I could do was shake my head and just as I was convinced that they were the most insane couple on Earth, Man-Man appeared in my doorway wearing an extra-large grin on his face; and I realized that my thoughts were wrong—they were even crazier. Hella strange.

I looked at Man-Man and for a moment I was convinced

he was an alien. "What. Are. You. Grinning. About?" I asked him.

"'Cause I can bounce in peace and don't have to worry about Pop calling my phone half the night and cussing me out." He revved invisible handlebars.

"Huh?" I blinked in disbelief. "Maybe it's just me but I could've sworn that you just begged her to get back together and then you topped it off by stalking her down the stairs, and practically out the door."

"I had to do that."

"Huh?"

"Look, Pop is my baby and breaking up and getting back together is how we do our thang. Which means that I know Pop well enough to know that if I didn't beg her back she would've stayed here extra long and tortured me with all kind of questions. '*Why you do this G? Why you do that?*' I'm allergic to questions like that."

"And what does that have to do with you begging for forgiveness?"

"Check it, if I beg her forgiveness, she'll think she has the upper hand, and that I'm over here losing it. Never in a million years would she think she was hitting me off with some peace."

"So you just played my girl? I don't appreciate that."

"Nah," Man-Man shook his head. "I love my boo, I just had wild oats to attend to and I didn't want her steppin' on my neck. Now look, my man, Ny'eem, is having a pickup game and I'm 'bout to get to it. You know a party ain't a party til G-Bread slide through. Now you wanna roll or tryna stay here and be in the lineup with Malik and the homework police?"

"I can't be with them alone. Oh, no."

"Thought so."

"But wait," I paused. "Did you say Ny'eem's game? Like the Ny'eem we know or another one."

"I only know one Ny'eem and yeah, he's having a pickup game. Now wassup, 'cause I'm 'bout to be out."

My heart thundered in my chest. I took a deep breath, and raced over to my full-length mirror. "Do I look okay?"

"Oh, here we go with that again." Man-Man shook his head. "Didn't I tell you to watch *Jersey Shore* if you looking for support? But I mean, you look a'ight. Just change those heels and put on some kicks."

"For what, it's his game not mine."

"'Cause heels in the park at a basketball game makes you look all desperate. Like a watered-down stripper ready to bust out."

"That sounds crazy."

"A'ight, chance if you want to, but don't get mad when dudes start calling you Candy-freak."

I hesitated and wondered for a moment if he was right. I didn't know, but something told me not to risk it. The last thing I wanted to look like was a watered-down stripper ready to make it happen.

I stood silent for a moment and then it hit me: it's eighty-five degrees outside and the perfect time for me to rock a pair of denim shorts, a hot pink spaghetti strap tee, and my Coach sneakers.

"I know you ain't about to change your clothes?" Man-Man complained as I flew past him and ran into the bathroom. "Dang!"

But I didn't care if he had an attitude, I had to get my

cute on. So, a half hour later my clothes were changed and my make-up was perfect.

"Can we roll now?" Man-Man asked, exhausted.

Before I answered I took one more peek in the mirror and confirmed my flyness. "Yep," I popped my glossy lips, "let's roll."

14

The evening sun sparkled like an amber diamond in the orange sky, as it hovered over the basketball court and set the mood for the illest basketball game I'd ever been to. And judging from all the cuties, the hotties, and the in-betweens, everybody knew this was the place to be.

Why?

'Cause the atmosphere was sick.

Dope.

And the basketball pounding against the black tarred court and swishing through the netted hoop with force was the music that everybody grooved to.

And the music was crazy.

There were two street teams made up of brown cuties—six feet tall and taller—and they were so fly that having all this fineness in one space was surreal. Unnatural. And all I wondered was: where have these ballers been all of my life?

I walked behind Man-Man and we eased onto the bottom bleacher and sat down. I nervously crossed one leg over the other as I watched Ny'eem dribble from the far end of the court, toward the basket. He spun around his guard, quickly flew through the air and slammed a layup!

Damn, he could ball.

And not only did I think so, the crowd did, too, because almost everybody in here lost it and cheered like crazy— except me.

I couldn't. I didn't want him looking my way and see my mouth gaped open. Suppose I had food on my teeth that I didn't know was there? How anti-fly would that be? Nah, I had to remain closed-mouth-glossy-lips-sexy. So I smiled...at least until I felt sweat bubbling on my forehead. Then, I almost fainted.

"Man-Man," I whispered.

"It's G-Bread."

Whatever. "Look, am I sweatin'?" I turned to face him and he frowned as he looked me over.

He shook his head and said, "Please, don't tell me you didn't put on any deodorant. Oh, this 'bout to be some bull." He sniffed. "Is that..." He sniffed again. "Is that you? Ahh damn." He held his index finger over his nostrils. "What the—!"

"Don't play me," I growled, smacking his hand down. "Be serious."

"I am serious." He looked me over. "Is that you?"

"O.M.G. No!"

"Oh," he said relieved. " 'Cause I was bout to say—!"

"Whatever. Just answer the question."

"Nah, you're cool. You ain't sweatin', but I am." He looked across the court, at a group of girls huddled in the corner. "I'm sweatin' like a pig in heat, 'cause those Nicki Minaj triplets got me feeling dirty." He fanned his face and shook his head. "Whew. 'Cuse me. I need to dip over there real quick." Without hesitation or any consideration for me, he strutted around the edges of the court, and left me sitting there solo.

I couldn't believe this. I felt like I was straight up on Broadway.

I should've called Pop and had her meet me here.

I let out an exhausted sigh.

Just chill and watch the game.

I watched the ball get passed around, snatched, and slung in the basket. Every time one of the players scored, the crowd screamed and chanted. *"Do, do, do ya thing! Ah work it out! Ah work it out!"*

I loved every moment of it and just as my nerves took a rest and the ever-ready butterflies in my stomach had fallen asleep, Ny'eem turned to make a layup and spotted me.

My heart dropped to my stomach.

And although Ny'eem only stared at me for a millisecond it felt like forever and ever...

I gave him a small wave and he returned a soft wink.

Don't ask me why, really don't, but suddenly I felt sooo silly that I giggled. Uncontrollably. Out of nowhere I burst into a low SpongeBob type laugh, like WTH was that?

Incredibly whack.

I did my best to collect myself. The girls, who sat next to me, took side glances at me, like they were waiting for me to freak out and really go crazy.

But I didn't. I pulled my shoulders back and resumed watching Mr. Wonderful work it out on the court.

Swish! The ball sailed through the basket. Ny'eem retrieved it. He dribbled with his left hand then switched to his right. "Am I in this alone?" he spat, talking smack. "Or did somebody else come to play with me? 'Cause if not, I can go home." He passed the ball to his teammate.

Ny'eem's teammate took a shot and made it. "There it is, baby!" Ny'eem shouted. "I see you came to play!"

Swish!

Ny'eem raced beneath the basket and grabbed the ball.

His guard reached in to take the ball and I yelled, "Reaching! Fall back! Not!" And when the ref didn't at least warn the player, I sucked my teeth and said, "This is some bull!"

"Eww," the girl sitting next to me said, "First Sponge-Bob and now you're an Angry Bird. Like really? Seriously? Could you please quiet down?" She rolled her eyes, turned to her friend who sat on the opposite side of her, and said, "Hood buggers."

My neck whipped toward them so fast that I almost caught whiplash. "Hood bugger?" I curled my lip. "Oh, you got me all the way messed up. Let me—"

"Foul!" The ref yelled and I completely lost the roll of words I was prepared to sting this wrecked-chicken with. "Pause," I said to her and held one finger up. Then I quickly returned my attention back to the game.

"Foul?!" I said to no one in particular, looking over the court. "Who fouled?" That's when I saw Ny'eem walk over to the foul line and prepare to take a shot. He looked so fine standing there; problem was his position was off. I wanted to yell, "Bend your knees!" But I didn't. Instead I watched him miss two free throws.

I should've said something.

The game was back in motion. "I see you," Ny'eem's guard spat, mad.

"Instead of seeing me, you need to be guarding me!" Ny'eem said.

And I shouted, "That's right, baby!" Realizing that I'd lost my mind, again. I didn't even look around, especially since I could feel at least ten pairs of eyes on me. But whatever, basketball was an emotional sport, and I was all in. Plus the cutie that I was diggin' was playing his heart out.

Ny'eem's guard slyly grabbed the ball and shot it down the other end of the court. The enemy scored but that was okay, things happen—but never fear 'cause my boo was near. He worked his way through center court, took the ball, and murdered a three-pointer.

"Yes!" I yelled, turned to the girl sitting next to me and held my hand up for a high-five. Then it clicked, that I wasn't clicking with this chick, so what the heck was I doing? I turned away from her with the quickness and resumed getting my basketball-boo-lovin' on.

The game was down to a minute left.

The score was tied.

Ny'eem had the ball. He dribbled it, stopped, and squatted to make a shot.

Don't do it, I thought as I stood up. My heart pounded in my stomach.

It's too risky. I sucked in a breath. I was sweatin' for sure now. I knew this could go one of two ways. If Ny'eem cared more about being a superstar than he cared about the game then he would take the shot. *But* if he cared more about the game then he would pass the ball off to his teammate who was closest to the basket.

I didn't know which one he would choose. All I knew was that I was getting anxious with each passing second.

The crowd cheered.

I bit into my bottom lip.

Ny'eem hesitated.

Ugg.

He passed the ball.

Yes!

His teammate caught it and slammed it through the basket!

Everybody screamed! Some people even jumped from their seats and raided the court. This was the best game I'd ever been to! 'Cept my own of course.

After being Ny'eem's sideline cheerleader and practically cussing out the broad sitting next to me, I now sat quietly in the stands and watched the court quickly turn from housing a hot game to housing a hot party. Some dude had an old school boom box, as big as a dorm room refrigerator. He amped it up and within an instant J. Cole's "Cole World" had this place on and crackin'.

Ny'eem stood on the court and there was a small cheering crowd standing around him, all giving him his props on a fierce game.

My stomach twisted in knots as I made up my mind to be bold, rise from my seat, and walk close to where he stood. I didn't want to mingle in with the crowd, mostly because I was nervous enough, I didn't need other people witnessing it.

Nyeem looked my way and his eyes smiled. "A'ight, yo," Ny'eem said to the crowd that surrounded him, "I'll get up." He exchanged a few more pounds and then he turned away and walked over to me.

Deep breath in... deep breath out...

I smiled and without my permission my hand gave him this hardy wave—which completely went south, because the wave should've only been a small and cute wave. Not one that looked as if I was fanning out a flame.

Shoot me.

Ny'eem gave me a crooked grin, which sank only one of his dimples. He softly flicked my chin and said, "So wassup?" His voice was oh soooo sexy. It took everything in me not to overheat.

"Nothing. The sky I guess." *Did I say that? Really? Now was not the time to say something soooo dumb! I wouldn't be surprised if he walked away. Matter of fact, I'll just count the seconds until he bolts outta here... one ... two...*

"I'm not talking about the sky," he said and instead of doing the expected two-step, he continued, "I'm talking about you—"

I know. "Oh, you're talking about me?"

"Yeah," he said. "Now tell me what's good with you? I gave you my number a minute ago. And I called you like two days in a row and you never called me back. I mean, it's cool, but you could've told me straight up if you didn't want to be bothered."

"It's not that," I said without thinking.

"Then wassup?"

Wassup is that every time I picked up the phone to call you, I froze and forgot the conversation that I'd practiced in my head. But I didn't say any of that, instead I said, "Has it really been that long? Oh my." I placed my hand on my chest and clutched invisible pearls.

Ny'eem looked at me like I was as crazy as I felt and

said, "A'ight. I see you playin' and since I just finished a game, I'ma catch you later." He hit me with a two-finger peace sign and walked away. Leaving me to wonder if my knees would withstand the embarrassment.

O.M.G. Am I dreaming? I pinched myself. I wasn't dreaming—I was screwing up my reality.

I watched Ny'eem walk past a few people, including Man-Man, give them dap, and then walk out of the court.

Follow him.

He already thinks I'm nuts, I don't need him thinking I'm a stalker.

Just chance it...

The soles of my sneakers skated like sandpaper across the court and down the tree-lined path, as I did my best to catch up with Ny'eem. Once I was a few inches away from him, I stopped and called his name: "Ny'eem!"

He kept walking.

And just when I was torn on whether to call him again or leave it alone and walk away, he turned around and faced me. "What?"

Just say it. "Can you come here for a minute?" I asked him.

"No," he said. "I'm not chasing you anymore. You wanna talk, you come to me." He continued walking, but he did slow down a little.

I swallowed as I caught up to Ny'eem and started walking alongside of him. I fiddled with my index finger, swallowed, and said, "Look, I had a long day. Fa' real. Nothing went as planned, including this moment. And it's not that I didn't want to call you or talk to you." I paused. *Spit it out.* "I just didn't know what to say to you."

"You could've started with 'hey wassup.' "

"True." I hunched my shoulders. "But I guess I didn't think about that."

"Maybe you think too much."

"Maybe I do."

"Maybe you just need to chill."

"Wow," I said. "Twice in one day."

"Huh? What happened twice in one day?" Ny'eem stopped for a moment and turned to me. "Somebody else told you to chill?"

I kicked bits of brittle branches and litter with my feet. "Yeah, my bff."

"Maybe you should listen?" We started slowly walking down the tree-lined path again.

"Maybe." I shrugged.

"Enough with the maybes and just do it."

I stopped and looked Ny'eem in the eyes. "It's not that easy for me. My life is different."

"Different how?" He turned to me.

I swallowed. "Look," I said with a little more attitude than I should've. "I'm not from the burbs, or this la-la side of Brick City. I'm from across town, where all the daddies are made of thin air, the mamas get high, and all the kids go to foster care. And the family I live with, psst, please, they aren't related to me. They're my foster family. I just met them a few weeks ago. And every time I thought about calling you I didn't know how to tell you that...or if I wanted to tell you that."

"Why not?"

"Because it made me feel weird. How was I supposed to say to a dude that I'm checking for that I'ma foster kid? Talk about killing the mood."

"You just say it."

"So I should've called you and said, 'Hey, Ny'eem, you remember me? I'm Gem and I'm homeless.'"

He chuckled a bit. "You're not homeless."

"I'm living someplace that's not my home."

"That's 'cause you won't make it your home. Are you cool where you're at or it's a problem?"

"No. It's no problem. They're good people."

"Then chill. Stop trying to predict the future. Trust me, just let it go."

"See you don't understand—"

"Gem," he reached for my hand. "My life hasn't been perfect either. My mother was on drugs ever since I could remember and she didn't get clean until recently."

I couldn't believe that. "What?" I said taken aback. "Seriously?"

"Word. My moms did her thing for a while. I mean, she's clean now, but when she was in the streets it was hell."

I giggled, and not the stupid SpongeBob giggle, a nervous one. "So having a mama strung out in the streets isn't exclusive to my neighborhood?"

He laughed a little. "Nah, y'all don't have that on lock. Sorry."

I smiled so hard, it's a wonder my teeth didn't fall out. "But, Ny'eem, the difference between me and you is that my mom doesn't wanna get clean."

"That's not the difference. The difference is that I knew I had to make my own way and I did. I didn't do pity parties, I took care of myself, and no, I didn't always make the best choices, which is how I ended up in juvy."

"Juvy? Like kiddy jail? Oh, you a real bad boy, huh? My James Dean." *Dumb...dumb...dumb...I just get dumber by the moment. If he walks away this time, I'ma just let him go.*

To my surprise Ny'eem didn't walk away. "I can only be your James Dean," he said, "if you pick up the phone and call me."

Freeze. Collect yourself, and don't say anything stupid. "I'ma call you. I promise."

"A'ight, we'll see," he said as we started our stroll again.

After a few moments of silence I said, "If you don't mind me asking, what did you go to juvy for?"

"Stealing cars."

"Stealing cars?" I was stunned. "Let me find out you stalking people's keys." There was my mouth again, out of control. "I'm sorry, I shouldn't have said that."

"It's cool," he smiled. "Because I didn't have to stalk keys. If I wanted a car I took it. Period, that was the point of being a car thief. I wasn't nice about it."

"Oh dang, it was like that?"

"Pretty much, until I got caught and was facing charges and double digit numbers."

"Wow. So what happened?"

"I plead guilty and the court offered me a first offenders juvenile program. I lived in a halfway house for a year."

"Seriously?"

"Yeah, that's where I met my mentor, Josiah. He plays college ball for Stiles U in New Orleans."

"I know who you're talking about!" I said excited. "He owns college ball. Fa' real, he stays on ESPN."

"Yeah," Ny'eem smiled proudly. "That's him. And believe it or not but Josiah was the first person to ever take me to a real basketball court."

"Fa'real?"

"Yup. And after a while, when I realized that I had talent on the court, I knew I had a choice: grinding or giving in. And since I wasn't about to give in, I got my grind on. And the next thing I knew I was being recruited by one of the top high schools in the country. And the rest is history."

"So are you tryna make it to the NBA?"

"Nah, Pretty Girl." He stopped walking and turned to look at me. "I'm just tryna make it."

Silence. I wanted to say something—scratch that—I wanted to say a million things and ask him a million questions, but I didn't, because suddenly it clicked to me that he pretty much told me the same things that Pop did. So maybe, maybe they were on to something. And if I wanted something different out of this place, this life, and this new zone I was tossed into, then I had to take it and make it work. I had to grind.

Hating that awkward moment of silence that had slid in between us I said, "So, what's a good time to call you?"

"Whenever you're ready."

"I'm ready now."

"Oh really?" He grabbed my hand and we locked fingers. "Straight."

I blushed. "I'm glad I came to see your game."

"Me too," he said.

"And speaking of the game I just have one lil thing I want you to do differently the next time."

"Oh, what you a coach now? Can you at least be my girl first, before you start directing my skills?"

His girl? Did he say his girl? Umm...am I melting? "Being your girl," I said brazenly, "has nothing to do with me noticing your skills. I'd be your girl even if I didn't know a thing about ball. But, since I do I just wanna tell you that the next time you're at the foul line, bend your knees."

"Bend my knees? What?"

"I'm just sayin'. Every other part of your game is tight. Straight. But your free throwin' is a little Shaq-esque."

He laughed. "So what you sayin', you could take me?" He wrapped his arms around my waist and gathered me close.

"Yeah," I said, dissolving into his embrace. "I would definitely take you." I slid my arms around his thick neck.

"Then when are you coming for me?" He softly placed his lips against mine.

"Now," I said as we kissed passionately, for what felt like an eternity.

15

A week later

Ever since Ny'eem asked me on a date—our first official date and not the lil Robin Hood run-ins we've had, but a date—the lyrics to Ciara's "C.R.U.S.H." were stuck in my head.

It was like...like...I had musical Tourette's. Because every time I turned around I was out of control and singing this song at the top of my lungs.

Sicko.com.

Imagine this: the other night at dinner and in the middle of Cousin Shake's hour-long tirade better known as grace, this song popped in my head and flew out of my mouth! I did a Beyoncé dip, snaked back up, and topped it off with, *"He's a keeper!"*

O.M.G.

It took me hella long—like two hours long—to explain to Cousin Shake and Ms. Minnie that I was not secretly sweatin' Cousin Shake. They made me raise my hand and take an oath that they were family and family didn't get "busy" like that.

Ewww.

Gag me. Seriously.

I was done. And although I stopped singing during dinner, I did hum. But that didn't settle Ms. Minnie because she still gave me extra hard side-glances—that clearly said she wouldn't hesitate to drop down a smack-down over Cousin Shake.

S.M.H.

I felt like there was a spell over me because the mere thought of Ny'eem sent tingling chills from my big toes to my eyebrows, forcing me to borderline on passing out.

Maybe I was possessed.

Yeah, that was it. Someone else had invaded my body, 'cause this person I took quick peeks at in the mirror was nothing like the Gem I knew.

This was some serious and for a moment I wondered if I needed crush-sick rehab. 'Cause there was no way in H to the double ell that this was normal; or that I should've been trippin' this hard over a 6' 2" cutie—I mean he did put all the hotties who'd ever lived to sleep. And he was soooo fine that his name should've been Fine. And yeah I love the way he texted me:

Yo, pr3tty girl, w3 shld chill 2g3th3r on day 6. Hang and hit up a spot 2 g3t some food.

Hellafied sexy. Especially the way he used 3's for E's.

But still...I had to have some kinda trippin' disorder to be going this hard.

Right?

Right.

As "C.R.U.S.H." blasted from my iPod and through my room I sorted through the mountain of clothes I'd dumped on my bed in frantic search of something fly to wear—which was turning out to be an epic fail. A dud. Everything that was cute and fly yesterday was today's hot mess. And I couldn't go see my cutie dressed in a hot mess. No way. No how.

I stood at the foot of my bed and then suddenly and without warning I stomped my feet like a five-year-old and screamed, "I'm not going!" And then I passed out, face first, into the heap of clothes spread across my bed.

"Woman down," I mumbled into a pair of True Religion jeans. "Code blue."

There was no coming back from this and the only thing on my mind was what would be in my eulogy.

Knock...knock...

I turned my head toward my door.

Not only was my door—which I thought for sure I'd closed—wide open, but Toi stood there cracking up.

Can you say embarrassed? Oh, I wanted to slam her in the face!

"I *know* my door was closed," I snapped, annoyed.

"No it wasn't," Toi said as she shook her head. "It was cracked. And when I heard you go from having a Ciara concert to having a love seizure I had to watch."

"Whatever."

"You may as well drop the extra, because I'm not leaving so don't even ask me to." The soles of Toi's leopard slippers slapped across the floor as she invited herself further into my room and lay on my bed face up and next to me—putting her butt directly on top of my ripped jeans and her head on my Hollister T-shirts and camisoles.

"So what's his name?" she asked. "And don't tell me none of my business. Oh and is he a cutie? For instance is he a milk chocolate brownie or a red velvet one with freckles sprinkled on his face. Or is he a butter pecan Latin cutie—Mr. Boneeeetaaah. Or are we takin' it all the way to the other side and got us, I mean, you, a hot lil cream-puff boo. All right now. Does he look like Justin Bieber?"

"Ill, no." I frowned.

"Ill? What you mean, ill? Bieber-boo is cute."

"So not my type."

"So what's your type?" She arched her brow. "Or better who's your type?"

I blushed. "I don't think you would know him even if I told you."

"It doesn't matter whether I know him or not. Just tell me."

I hesitated. Since I'd been here Toi and I had barely said two words to one another so I wasn't exactly sure if I needed to be blabbing all my business to her. I cleared my throat.

"Are you worried I'ma tell Mommy?" Toi asked before I could say anything. "I'm the last one you have to worry about. Seven is the dry snitch—she'll have your business all through the house. I'm the calm twin—well sort of. But still you can trust me not to tell Mommy. You see I have a son, right?"

"Yeah."

"Well, I had him at sixteen by a weed pusher turned deadbeat baby daddy."

"Fa'real?"

"Yup. And Mommy tried to stop my madness by running up in his crib like at three in the morning and dragging me out. But by the time she did that I was already pregnant. Needless to say I have done so much dirt that I'm the last one to go around selling out your drama to Mommy. Now give me his stats."

"He's no big deal."

"He's big enough of a deal to be lying on a pile of clothes moaning."

"I wasn't moaning."

"You *were* moaning. And another thing, I'm starting to feel some kind of way that you only want to hang with Man-Man, but are always on the defense with me. Wassup with that?"

I shrugged. "I don't know. I guess half the time I'm trying to figure out why you're being so nice to me. Like whatchu you want?" *I'm not sure if I should've said that or not, but, oh well.*

"Man-Man is nice to you, too. And you don't think he wants anything."

"Man-Man's not nice to me. He's using me to pull girls."

Toi chuckled. "You know he likes you."

I smiled, a small smile, but it was still a smile. Well sort of. "Yeah, maybe."

"Well, maybe I like you, too, and I would like to be your big sister if you would give me the time of day. Unless you think I'm incredibly corny or whack or something."

After the story you just told me about your life I don't think you're incredibly corny or whack. Well, not anymore . . .

"You're okay," I said.

"Well, since I'm okay, then tell me who's Mr. Boo, 'cause I wanna know."

"Okay," I swallowed, hoping to keep the butterflies down. "Okay, he's one of Man-Man's friends."

Toi's eyes bugged. "Somebody from the broke-down-crew? Oh no, we don't do broke boys. We start thinking about credit and bank accounts early."

I laughed. "He is sooooo not about the busted life. He works and goes to school. He's only Man-Man's boy, he's not Man-Man."

"Oh, okay. Now what's his name?"

"Ny'eem."

"Ny'eem." She snapped her fingers, as if she were trying to flick on a light switch. "Ny'eem...Ny'eem...Oh, lil fine Ny'eem. Mr. Hershey Bar basketball player. Hey-hey-now! Lil Wale in the house!"

I was grinning so hard it's a wonder the weight of my smile didn't sink me through the mattress. "Yeah, that's him. Party ovah here!" I said being unexpectantly silly.

Toi and I laughed. Then I let out an exhausted sigh and rolled over on my back. "We're supposed to go to the Meadowlands Fair tonight, but I don't think I'm going," I said.

"Why?"

"'Cause I have nothing to wear."

"Nothing?" She looked confused. "We're lying on a mountain of clothes."

"And not one thing is hot."

Toi sat up and looked toward my skimpy closet and shook her head. "Maybe we ought to sort through what we're lying on."

"I already did, they're garbage. Hot trash. I'd be flyer dressed as a Hefty CinchSak."

She laughed. "Girl, get up and let's see what we can find that's cute."

Toi and I slid off the bed and she sorted through the mountain of clothes.

She picked up a pair of True Religion skinny jeans, a slouchy beige shirt with a black sequin cross going down the middle, and a black camisole.

Oh, that's cute.

"Here, try this on," Toi said.

I quickly changed into the outfit, turned toward Toi and she said, "Let's find something else."

"Yeah." I frowned. "Told you, nothing to wear."

She sorted through my clothes and picked out a pair of black leggings and a sleeveless top that stopped midway down my thighs. I changed and walked over to my full-length mirror. I looked at Toi whose reflection was behind mine and we said simultaneously, "Not."

"I give up." I threw my hands in the air.

"Don't. Try this." She handed me a pair of black Forever 21 destroyed skinny jeans, a white mid-drift top with a hood and the words "Live in the Now" written in sparkling black letters, and a black camisole to wear beneath the mid-drift. I slipped the clothes on and as I walked toward the mirror she said, "Umm, wait. Don't look in the mirror yet, stand there." She ran into her room and came back with a handful of jewelry, a comb, brush, and make-up. "Sit down." She pointed to my computer chair.

I sat down and said, "I wanna see how I look."

"Just wait. Let me finish hooking this up. I think this may be the one." She handed me a pair of large silver hoops, matching chunky bangles, and then she proceeded to pull my hair into a side ponytail that dangled over my right shoulder. She put a little make-up on me: eye shadow, liner, and gloss. "Wait, the shoes!" she said. Toi chose my four-inch black peep toe platforms. She placed her hands on her hips and stood back. "There it is, fly girl. Now check it out!"

I walked over to the mirror not knowing what to expect, but the moment my reflection lit up the glass I knew this was it. "This is fly!" I turned around and gave her a high five. "Yeah, you did this!" I turned back toward the mirror, puckered my lips, and blew myself a kiss.

I'm not sure what came over me, all I knew is that I was poppin' it in my too cute outfit and Toi was like, "Go, Gem! It's ya birthday! You gon' get your date on like it's ya birthday!"

"Oh hell nawl, Broke Down!" Cousin Shake barged into my room. "Toi, I told your mama you hadn't changed and couldn't be trusted! Oh Lord!" he shouted.

"What?" She looked at him like he was even crazier than usual. "What are you talking about?"

"Broke Down, why you trying to turn out Lil Project?"

Did he just call me a project? Cousin Shake must've read my mind because he looked at me and said, "Yeah, I called you a project. 'Cause somebody need to fix you. Your mouth's nasty, your eyes stay rollin', and your teeth stay smackin'. So yeah, I said it. Lil Project. Under Con-struc-tion." He bucked his chest up. "And what!"

I didn't even respond to him and all Toi did was roll her eyes toward the ceiling. "Cousin Shake!" Malik ran into my room. "I just told him to assume position. His nose and his palms should be touching the wall!"

"Who?" Toi frowned.

"The guy who just showed up for Gem, Ny'eem!" Malik

laughed and in between thoughts of wanting to fly kick him all over the room all I saw when I stared at him was a mini Cousin Shake.

Not wanting to stand here a moment longer Toi and I hurried out of the room and once I stood in the middle of the staircase I was able to see that Ny'eem wasn't in position, instead he looked up the stairs and smiled at me.

My heart thundered.

He was so fine that I lost control of my lips and smiled from ear to ear. Cousin Shake walked past me and said, "Close your mouth."

Grrrrr...

Cousin Shake walked over to Ny'eem and said, "Wassup, son?"

"You got it, sir," Ny'eem said. "How are you this evening?"

"How I am depends on how you bringin' it?"

Ny'eem chuckled. "I'm good, Cousin Shake."

"My name was Cousin Shake when you were coming over here kicking it with the G-beg."

"It's G-Bread," Malik corrected Cousin Shake.

"Whatever," Cousin Shake snorted and continued, "But now that you're here to see one of my girls my name has changed and you need to call me Mr. M.C. Ole G and Chocolate."

"What?" Me and Toi said simultaneously.

Where was Ms. Grier when I needed her?

Cousin continued, "So let me put you up on how I get down."

"Break it down, Big Homie." Malik cracked his fat knuckles.

"Would you two stop it?" Toi said.

"Seriously," I said with my lips tight.

Cousin Shake ignored us and carried on, "Now check it, do you know how special it is and what it means to take one of my girls out the house?"

I could tell Ny'eem wanted to laugh but he didn't, and instead he said, "It means I have to take care of her and show her a nice time."

"Hell nawl!" Cousin Shake snapped. "It means is that she ain't no hoochie—'cause we don't come from that. So don't have her out there grindin' and poppin' it. 'Cause her name ain't Dollar Bill, Peaches, Don't-Stop-Get-it-Get-it, or Cookie, smell me?"

"Yes, sir," Ny'eem said, still doing his best not to laugh.

"We cool then, Bruh." Cousin Shake shook Ny'eem's hand and then patted him on the back. Afterward he walked up to me and whispered, "Gem, I want you to make sure you keep a watch on him. Now take this money and keep it in your pocket just in case you need anything." He handed me a dollar bill. "Use it wisely."

All I could do was shake my head. Cousin Shake was nutz. Completely delusional.

"Next time," I whispered to Ny'eem, "wait outside, I'll jump out the window."

"What you say, Lil Project?" Cousin Shake snorted.

My name was not Lil Project. "All I said was..." I paused and quickly decided against spewing the sarcastic remark I was about to say. Hmph, I was almost out the door and there was no need in pushing Cousin Shake into completely flipping out. The last thing I wanted to see was his Running Man and cat daddy routine. So I swallowed my smart remark and said, "I'm just sooo happy that you came inside to meet my family."

"Yeah." Ny'eem smiled. "They're cool people." He reached for my hand and instantly chills ran through me. Ny'eem looked me over. "You look fly, Pretty Girl."

I blushed. "Thank you."

"So are you ready?" he asked.

"Yeah, I'm ready."

Ny'eem walked toward the front door and I walked behind him. I waved and smiled at Toi, slyly pumped my fist at Malik, and I started to roll my eyes at Cousin Shake, but quickly changed my mind. I gave him a small wave instead and then I walked out behind my baby.

16

The carousel Ny'eem and I rode on had spinning lights that flashed through the night's sky like a colorful burst of Heaven. We sat on a crisp white, high-back bench, in between the porcelain unicorns and horses, eating cotton candy from the same stick. He was so cute as I took pieces of the soft pink candy and slipped them into his mouth, purposely letting my index finger stroke the center of his tongue.

"Yo," he said as the carousel spun softly. "Don't tell anybody that you were feeding me cotton candy, a'ight?"

"Why?" I blushed, as I snuggled against his chest and he clasped his hands around my waist. "It's romantic."

"Being here with you is romantic. You feeding me cotton candy—pink cotton candy—is a little you know..."

"No, what?"

"A little," he hesitated. "You know—"

"Anti-swag?" I volunteered.

"There it is."

I laughed as I ran my thumb across his full lips and swept away a few specks of sugar. "Ooooh, sooo, you have to keep your thuggism in check at all times. Got it."

"Don't be extra." He smiled at me and I wanted to melt.

"I'm not being extra. I gottchu, boo. I. Gottchu."

He laughed and leaned in for a kiss. I gave him a soft peck on the lips and he said, "Yeah, if I'm riding a merry-go-round and you're feeding me cotton candy, you got me for sure."

My heart skipped not one but three beats and I settled even deeper into his chest. He caressed the side of my hair and all I could do was close my eyes and get lost in the soft feel of his hands.

I felt like I was riding on a cloud and I never wanted to get off. Ever.

Who knew that being at the Meadowlands Fair would feel like this? Like the best thing I'd ever experienced. And maybe that's why I felt a little weird—just a little—because I had no idea how I'd ever come off of a high like this. This had to be what the best movie scenes were made of; and what walking heartbeats felt like.

Mesmerized.

Hypnotized.

Awestruck.

Beaming from the right side of Cupid.

This was the bomb.com and I was basking in the explosion of it all.

After our carousel ride we strolled through the fair hand in hand. There were people everywhere. The concession stands were packed and the lines that led to the rides were wrapped around corners. There were a ton of booths all with carnival games and plush prizes of stuffed animals that dangled from the booths' ceilings. And just when I thought that the evening couldn't possibly be any more romantic, Ny'eem pointed to the house of mirrors and said, "Let's go in here."

And we did.

And we got lost in a sea of our reflections.

It was the prettiest thing I'd ever seen. Ny'eem was everywhere all at once and for the first time in my life I knew that I wanted things to stay this way.

Once we found our way out of the maze of mirrors we resumed our stroll and talked about everything—school, movies, friends, family, relationships, basketball. I told Ny'eem how much I loved ball, but all the reasons I gave up on it. And I told him that I'd never really kicked it with a boo like this, because I'd always had too many other things going on—but that for the first time ever, I felt like I could take a deep breath and exhale. Really, really, let it all go.

And I guess Ny'eem felt pretty comfortable with me too because he also confided things in me. Like, although he was seventeen, he had his own spot because his family moved out to L.A. so that his sister could pursue her singing career, but that he stayed behind in their old place. He told me that he missed them, but that he couldn't follow his sister's dreams, because he had to follow his own, which were here in Brick City.

And not only did we share serious things, but we were silly, too. And not a nervous silly. But the kind of silly that made each other's faces light up when we laughed.

This was perfect.

Flawless.

"Hold up," I said to Ny'eem, stopping us dead in our

tracks. I pointed to a booth with two basketball hoops and stuffed animals hanging from the ceiling. "We're at a fair, so—"

"So what?" he gloated. "You want me to win you a prize?" *Oh, no he didn't.*

His cockiness continued. "What you want, the biggest bear up there?"

I laughed. "Lil Shaq, puhlease. You do know those are free throws and not layups, right?"

"Oh, you tryna play me, Pretty Girl?" He chuckled.

"Oh no, baby. I'm just keeping it real. You couldn't win me a prize from there, but I most certainly could win you one. Matter of fact, I could win you two." I stroked his chin. "Now which bears do you want, the lil yellow ones? Oh wait, you have to keep your thug-thizzle straight so I'm sure you want the blue ones."

"Funny. And you're talking an awful lot of smack, but I don't see you stepping over there to bring it. Oh wait, I forgot," he smirked. "You gave up on ball."

"Oh, you really went there?"

"It is what it is, Baby Girl," he continued. "I'm still feeling you though, even if you are scared."

"Scared. Boy please, I can bring it."

"Bring what, my towel to the locker room?" he laughed.

I playfully mushed him in the center of his chest. "Five dollars says I can bring it all day." I stepped over to the booth and took position behind the basket to the right.

"Yeah, a'ight, and ten dollars says you can't." He took position behind the basket to the left.

The guy running the game booth said, "You two up?"

"Yup," I said, filled with confidence, while reaching in my purse for money. "And this game's on me."

"Nah," Ny'eem said, "I got it." He placed two dollars on the counter.

"Oh, you're just gon' give away all ya lil money, huh?"

He chuckled. "Nah, I'm just trying to make sure you'll have the money you're about to owe me."

"Whatever." I picked up one of the balls and aimed it toward the basket.

"Let's get it," Ny'eem said.

The game booth worker nodded his head and said, "One, two, three, go!"

"Yo, Pretty Girl, I think you cheated," Ny'eem said, handing me the ten dollars he'd lost.

I chuckled. "Yeah, you and Man-Man are definitely friends, because he said the same thing when I beat him. Now, boo-boo, which bear do you want?" I pointed toward the assortment of bears in the booth.

"Let's see here," the game booth worker said. "We have, ahh, a nice sunshine yellow one here, a lil rainbow-colored bear—"

"Yo," Ny'eem said. "What I look like, picking out a stuffed bear? You got a toy gun?"

"A toy gun?!" I laughed so hard I cried. "You have lost your mind. They don't have any toy guns." I looked at the game booth worker—who, judging by the look on his face, thought we were both crazy. "I'll take the pink one," I said.

"Yeah, you do that," Ny'eem said as the guy handed me the bear and I laughed for at least ten more minutes.

"You finished with the joke?" Ny'eem asked, which caused me to laugh even more. He looked down at me and he was trying his best to hold a serious face. It didn't work, and he ended up with a wide smile across his lips.

"Don't be mad," I said. "Gimme kiss." And he did.

For the next hour we walked around the fair, rode the Ferris wheel, ate hotdogs, funnel cakes, and freshly fried donuts. By the time we were leaving I knew for sure that I'd had the best time of my life.

We held hands as Ny'eem drove me home and by the time he pulled up and parked in front of the house, I closed my eyes and wished that we could rewind time and relive tonight all over again.

Ny'eem softly turned my face toward him. "Let me rap to you real quick."

I squeezed his hand and said, "Wassup?"

He stroked his goatee and said, "Yo, tonight was cool."

"Really?" I blushed.

"Yeah, Pretty Girl. I enjoyed it, ma."

"I enjoyed tonight too, poo."

He gave me half a smile. "So then maybe we're thinking the same thing, 'cause I'm thinking that I'd like to do more than kick it."

Is he about to ask me to move in with him? If so I'll go and pack my clothes right now. "What are you thinking?" I asked him.

"I'm thinking I want you to be my girl. How do you feel about that? Is that a'ight with you?"

I didn't open my mouth. I couldn't. Because I knew if I did I'd either ask him to marry me or I'd be stuttering all over myself.

"Talk to me," he said, flicking my chin.

"Umm..." I paused. "Are you serious?"

"Always."

Again, I hesitated, but this time I did it intentionally. This way he would think there was a possibility I would say no. Not that I would. But he didn't need to know that.

Seems my hesitation worked because he said, "Whatever you decide is cool. If the answer is no I'll understand."

Boy, I could never tell you no. "It's not that the answer is no," I said. "It's just that I've been single for soooo long..." I got that line from a movie and I stopped myself mid-sentence because I couldn't remember the rest of it. "And umm..." *Dang, what is the rest of that line? I guess I better freestyle.* "And umm, I had a really good time with you tonight."

"And?" he pressed.

"And umm..." I paused again. *Just say yes. No, I can't, 'cause then I'll sound desperate. Should I put a spin on it? Yeah. Spin it.*

I turned and looked Ny'eem directly in his eyes and just as I opened my mouth to spin my version of yes I quickly changed my mind and decided to drop the game. "I'd love to be your girl," I said.

"Once you're my girl, you know I'ma keep you forever..."

I giggled. "Forever-ever."

"Yeah." Ny'eem smiled and moved in for a kiss. "Forever-ever."

"I think I should get going," I said, ending our kiss.

"Yeah, maybe so."

I gave him one last peck before walking up the stairs and putting a little extra bounce in my runway strut. Once I had my key in the door, I turned around and he was still standing there—leaning against the passenger door and watching me. I blew him a kiss and he gave me a soft wink.

My heart clapped in my chest, making me giggle nervously as I opened the door and stepped inside.

"Ah ha!"

I dropped my purse to the floor and practically fainted.

It was Malik. He'd sprung out of nowhere and scared the heck outta me!

"Are you crazy!" I snapped, storming past him and up the stairs to my room. "Why would you scare me like that?!" I walked into my room and kicked my shoes off.

Malik stood in the doorway and said, "You know Baby-Tot-Tot is about to turn you in, right?"

"What. Are. You. Talking. About?"

"Cousin Shake made me the house police!" he said proudly.

"So?"

"So, I'ma tell that you were bustin' out a lip-lock in front of the house with ole boy."

"I don't care what you tell Cousin Shake!"

"Cousin Shake?" He looked at me like I was crazy. "I'm not gon' tell Cousin Shake, I'ma tell the real Big Homie, Mommy!"

And before I could threaten his life he raced out of the room and down the stairs and that's when my thoughts suddenly switched from cutting Malik's time on Earth short to wondering when the heck did he start calling Ms. Grier "Mommy"....

17

"Deep breath in. Deep breath out. And focus," Ny'eem said, as we stood in the school's parking lot. We'd been kicking it straight and strong for a week and a half. The best week and a half of my life. And not just with Ny'eem, with everything.

Home.

School.

Friends.

True story, this new side of sixteen was the bomb. And I wasn't sure the exact day, time, or hour things had changed or when I'd dropped my hesitation. I just knew that my life felt different. My only worry now was that things really were what they seemed and I wasn't slippin'.

"Just chill and claim your zone," Ny'eem continued on with his pep speech. "Go in there and kill 'em! Don't be nervous at all. 'Cause you got this, Pretty Girl. It's our world—"

"Okay, Mr. Hype-man, can you stop?"

"Why?" he said, taken aback. "I'm just getting warmed up. I didn't practice basketball with you all week for nothing. We 'bout to take it all the way, baby! Go hard or sit down. And we don't sit down." He made an invisible three-point play. "'Cause we're too busy flying through the air. *Swish*...And the crowd goes wild!" he said excited. "Can't you just see it?"

"Yeah, umm hmm," I said, with as much sincerity as I could.

"Yo, what's that about?" Ny'eem leaned against the trunk of his car. "Talk to me."

I walked up close to Ny'eem and he placed his hands on my hips. I tilted my forehead into his hard chest and he placed his chin in the center of my head.

I wished I could share his excitement. But I was still a little iffy. Scratch that, I was hella iffy. And yeah, this was something that I wanted to do. And yeah, for the last week tryouts had been on my mind like crazy. But still, that didn't stop me from being nervous. "I'm just a little—" I said.

"Nervous," he said, finishing my sentence.

I shrugged. "Yeah."

"Look." Ny'eem kissed me in the center of my head. "You gon' have to man-up and dead the nerves."

"What?" I held my head up. I couldn't believe he said that.

"Real talk," he continued on. "I can't baby you right now and talk to you like Ny'eem the boyfriend. I have to kick it to you like Ny'eem the player. And I know that if you don't murder those nerves and start feelin' like you're the best player out there, you won't even get close to making the cut."

"Why would you say that? Dang, can I get some sympathy here?"

"Nah, sympathy is for the stands, not the court. So check it, you gon' have to shake the nerves so that you can go in there and prove yourself. Trust, even though those chicks will turn out to be your teammates, and they might come around and be nice eventually, they will be gunnin' for you initially. Especially the one who thinks you're going in there to jock her spot."

"I'm not trying to jock anybody's spot. I just wanna be a part of the team."

"Then pick your chest up and let's get it."

"You really think it's that simple?"

"It's gon' have to be."

Silence. Like what was I supposed to say? And maybe he was right, because the only thing being nervous did for me was make me sweat. And I hated to sweat unnecessarily.

I looked at my purple G-Shock sports watch. "Well, I guess I start gettin' it by being on time." I gave him a kiss good-bye and as I turned to walk away Ny'eem said, "Hol' up, ma. I have something for you. I almost forgot."

I glanced at my watch again; I had fifteen minutes to be on the court.

"It'll only take a minute," Ny'eem assured me.

"Okay, what is it?"

Ny'eem smiled as he opened his trunk and pulled out a Foot Locker bag. He handed it to me. "Thought you might like these."

I did all I could to control the squeal I felt bursting inside of me. But I couldn't, I had to let it out. So I squealed as I pulled a sneaker box from the bag, opened the box, and kaboom! There was a pair of black and white Nike Hyperdunks!

POW!

It was official, I was straight fly now. These kicks were just what I needed to send my confidence into overdrive. I quickly changed my sneakers and said, "Thank you, poo." I hugged him tightly.

"Thank me by making the team." He gave me a fist bump and I hurried across the lot.

Showtime...I thought as I approached the double doors that led to the gym. I took a deep breath as I stepped in. The buzzing sound of anxious players and the screeching sounds of their rubber soles filled my ears.

I spotted Pop immediately. She was suited up in orange basketball shorts, a white tank top, and black Nikes. We were almost dressed alike except my shorts were black and her Nikes were Jordans. I wondered what Pop would think once she saw me, especially since I didn't tell her that I'd be here. I walked carefully toward her. Her back was to me, her hands were on her hips, and her neck was doing what it did best—snaking from left to right. "This season is 'bout to be fiyah!"

"Yup." I bounced my way in front of her. "Especially since I'm here!"

"GEM!" she screamed, and jumped up and down, hugging me. "O.M.G.! I'm sooooo happy you're here! Girl, it's on fa'sho! Kamani, Janay, she came! Told y'all she wouldn't be able to resist staying away 'cause at the end of the day she's a what? A ball player." Pop twirled around and made an invisible layup. "Bam!"

After her celebration dance Pop introduced me to a few teammates as well as some of the other girls who were trying out. "The Rich Girlz 'bout to make it happen, boop!" Pop said excited.

For some reason Pop's comment about the Rich Girlz made me look directly in Kamani's face, who of all people had the nerve to have on the same sneakers as me. It took everything in me—or out of me, depending on how you looked at it—not to roll my eyes. "Nice sneakers, Kamani."

"Yeah." She gave me a tight smile. "My boo gave 'em to me. How you get yours? Donation?"

A few of the girls who stood around snickered, which made me really want to cuss Kamani out, but since I wasn't on the team and hadn't even officially tried out, I figured it was best not to bring the drama. So I decided to let Kamani's comment go. This time.

The coach, who could've easily passed for Lisa Leslie, walked over to me and said, "I'm Coach Rays and you are?" She tapped her pen on her pad as she waited for me to answer.

"Gem. Gem Scott."

She scribbled my name down and nodded. "All right. Well next time, be on time," she said.

"I thought tryouts started at four o'clock. It's four o'clock now." I pointed to the clock.

"Listen, if you wanna be on this team then you'll learn quickly that being on time means being here early."

I hoped this wasn't a bad sign. I tried to shake the thought. "My fault," I said. "Now I know."

She nodded again, sized me up, and looked over at Pop. "Is this the young lady you were telling me about, Cameron?"

"Yop," Pop said proudly.

Coach shot Pop a loaded eye and Pop quickly said, "I meant yes, Coach. This is Gem."

"What position are you aiming for, Gem?" Coach asked.

"Point guard."

"Well, best of luck," the coach said as she walked away and over to the assistant coach.

"She hates me," I said to Pop, shaking my head. "It took her two point five seconds to size me up and hate me."

"She doesn't hate you," Pop said. "She hates everybody. So don't worry about it. Just know that we 'bout to turn the heat up, baby!"

"Slow down, Pop," Kamani said. "Because first Gem needs to make the team."

Oule, I can't stand this chick. "I will," I said with confidence.

"Maybe," Kamani said. "But just so you know, the point guard position is sewed up. But there just might be a spot on the sidelines where you can be my cheerleader."

I snickered, mostly because if I didn't chop this chick up to being a joke I would steal on her. But don't get it twisted, although I laughed I had to say something because she'd already said something slick and got away with it. I couldn't let her get that off again. "Yeah, I know the point guard position is sewed up, 'cause I'm 'bout to take it."

"Umph," came from a few of the girls standing around.

"Girl, please," Kamani rolled her eyes at me. "You gon'

be so far down on the bench that you gon' need a walkie-talkie to even say hello to Coach."

"Oule…" Rang like a musical note from a few of the girls who'd been listening. And just as I went to put everybody in their places Coach blew her whistle and yelled, "Everybody on the line! It's time for suicides!"

18

I think I died every day after school.
Seriously.

Either that or Coach turned each of us into freaks for a week. She made us run from the front of the court to the back, from left to right, race to the center, jump twice, make a layup, and then start the death sprints all over again.

Can you say mad crazy?

Hellafied nutz.

I wasn't trying to be a track star. I just wanted to dribble a little bit, take it to the hoop, get the crowd hyped over a few unexpected three pointers, and then slam, bam, be a basketball star and go home—alive. Not murdered.

But obviously Coach Rays had other plans.

All I knew is that the list of who made the cut was to be posted on the gym's bulletin board in about—I looked at my watch—ten minutes and if I didn't make the team it was gon' be a problem. And no, I wasn't exactly sure how I was gon' bring it—being that Coach was 6' 3" and pretty much made two of me. All I knew is that somehow I was gon' lay it down.

Trust.

"My stomach has been in knots all day," Pop leaned over and whispered. "I need to know if you made the team."

Before I said anything I looked up at my English teacher, who on most days thought he was Shakespeare—and he was too busy putting on a fake British accent and reciting his favorite lines from *Romeo and Juliet* to pay us any attention. Needless to say the coast was clear for me to say, "My stomach has been in knots, too, Pop. That's all I keep thinking about. 'Cause fa'real, fa'real, I can't do another day of these tryouts—"

"Oh my God, Coach is going extra hard. Ever since one of the seniors got recruited last year and went straight to the WNBA, Coach has lost her mind."

"So she is crazy? I knew it."

"Crazy ain't the word. That's why, when my uncle brought her home last year and said she was his new boo, I flatlined."

"Whaaaat?!" I said a little too loud, which caused Mr. Simmons to look my way and shoot me the evil eye. He only shot me daggers for a few seconds though and then he returned to his British accent. "Pop," I whispered. "Coach Rays is your uncle's boo?"

"Yes, girl." Pop shook her head. "Family reunions will never be the same," she sniffed.

"I think we need a moment of silence for that one."

"Yeah," she sniffed again. "Let's bow our heads. 'Cause I really need to mourn this. And I don't even know how they hooked up, my uncle is only five-foot-six."

"What? That's like Kevin Hart dating Precious." I shook my head. "That's just wrong."

"Can you imagine what their kids will look like?" Pop said, disgusted.

"Yeah, we need an emergency moment of silence." We held our heads down for a second and I did my best to erase the visual of Coach Rays and her too-short boo.

Pop took a deep breath and I took that as a signal our moment of silence had ended.

"Any chance Coach is going to hang up the list early?" I whispered to Pop.

"Girl, please. She does everything by the book."

I looked at my watch and only five minutes had gone by. I swear time was dragging. "I wish this class would end already," I huffed.

"Me too," Pop agreed.

"I just want to know so bad if I made the team," I said. "But, for-real-for-real I'm glad tryouts are done because all I've been able to do this week when I got home was finish my homework and go to sleep."

"Word," Pop agreed.

"I haven't even had a chance to say more than hello and good-bye to my boo."

"Screetch!" Pop stood up, snapped her fingers, and said loud as ever, "Hold up, wait a minute—"

"Pop," I whispered, hoping to get her to calm down before the teacher turned around. "Would you sit down, you're too loud."

I'm thinking that the words "my boo" must've put Pop

in a trance because instead of calming down she got louder. "Hold up. Wait. A. Minute. Cameron 'Popcorn' Hunter is 'bout to put some push up in it!" She dropped to the floor and snaked back up. "Now wassup? When did you get a boo? And bigger than that when did you start keeping secrets from me?"

"That's a very good question, Ms. Hunter." Mr. Simmons cut his fake British accent short and returned to his American one. "Since you are obviously more invested in Ms. Scott's secrets than you are in what you'll be tested on, then why don't you tell us all about Ms. Scott's boo."

All I could do was shake my head.

"Okay, okay." Pop smacked her lips and said, "See, what had happened was I was comparing her to Shakespeare's Janette—"

"It's Juliet," I whispered.

"Yeah, Juliet and Raheem—"

"Romeo."

"Yeah him and—"

Bringggggg.

"Ups there's the bell," Pop said and we hurriedly tossed our books in our backpacks, shot Mr. Simmons a two-finger peace sign, and flew out the door. "Gotta go!"

"Whew, that was close," Pop giggled as we ran down the stairs and toward the gym. "But right after we find out if we have to run up on Coach or not we'll be getting back to your mysterious boo."

"Okay." I blushed as Pop and I hurried down the hall. There was a massive crowd standing around the glass-encased bulletin board. There were so many kids hovered around that for a moment it felt like teen night at the club, instead of an afternoon of "who made the cut." A few people bum rushed their way to the front of the crowd and others stood back and waited.

Me and Pop didn't have the patience to wait so we pushed our way to the front and shot looks that clearly dared anyone to say anything out of the way to us.

Sweat gathered on my forehead and ran down my temples. The list had to be typed in the tiniest font I'd ever seen, 'cause dang, I couldn't find my name anywhere. I tapped my index finger alongside of every name on the list and nothing. My name was nowhere. As a matter of fact I didn't recognize any of these names. My heart sank and I looked at Pop. Tears gathered in the corners of her eyes. "I know my daddy said that violence was never acceptable," Pop sniffed. "But we gon' have to jump that heifer now and repent later. Only thing is we might have to beat my uncle down, too."

"It's cool, Pop. It's no need to cause family drama 'cause I didn't make the team."

I bit the corner of my lip. I was doing all I could to fight back tears.

Pop draped her arm over my shoulders and said, "I don't care what you say, we three o'clockin' that trick."

"Excuse me, excuse me." Coach Rays cut through the crowd.

"You wanna jump her now?" Pop whispered.

I didn't answer, because although I knew it was wrong I was seriously thinking about laying Coach Rays down.

Coach Rays opened the bulletin board's glass case and pinned another typed list in the center, next to the one that was already there.

"Coach," Pop said. "You're posting two different lists of who made the cut? Is that something new?"

Coach looked at Pop, and I swear I don't think this woman ever blinked. "Cameron, the list I just posted is the basketball list. The other list," Coach pointed toward the bulletin board, "is for field hockey. I sure hope you two play better than you read," she said as she walked away.

Can you say duh?

Immediately my eyes scanned the basketball list and there it was—my name practically in lights! "Gem Scott—Point Guard." Pop must've spotted it at the same time, because she shouted and we hugged tightly.

Hands down, along with the day I became Mrs. Ny'eem, this was the best day of my life!

Pop and I walked into the crowded and chatter-filled cafeteria like we owned the spot. Four-inch stilettos that stepped heel to toe and hips that swayed from one end of the clock to the other. No one would ever know that my body was sore as heck from weeklong tryouts—and besides, I was on a diva's high and divas always rolled in stride.

We grabbed two lunch trays of turkey sandwiches, curly fries, and blond brownies. Afterward, we took a seat at our daily lunch table, next to the vending machines and the water fountain.

Not even two seconds after we sat down and I peeled the crust off of my sandwich did Pop start going in, "You gon' have to put the sandwich on pause, because I have to know now, who's the boo? And by the way, should we review the bestie rules? That I am to know everything. Let me rewind that er'thang. Like don't leave me out on nothing. If you sneeze I need to know what triggered it. Feel me? I'ma give you a Paris Hilton pass on that mishap, but the next time you will receive twenty-four hour bestie probation," Pop said, all in one breath. "Okay."

"Okay," I said, amazed that she didn't pause, not once. "My fault."

"Umm hmm." She shoved a curly fry into her mouth. "Now, let's start with his name, his crew, his age, how tall, his race, religion, j-o-b, what grade he's in. Where does he rate on the cuteness scale, and did he tell you he loved you yet?"

I blinked. I was convinced that spitting everything out in one breath must've been a talent. "Okay, on the cuteness scale he defies all numbers. Like straight up and off the charts."

"Snap-snap." Pop smiled.

"His name is Ny'eem."

"Awwwwl," she whined. "So when y'all get married and have a baby, you could name your daughter Ny'eema and your son Gem. That would be so hot."

"Who's getting married?" Kamani asked. She and Janay had just walked over to the table and sat down.

"Gem's getting married," Pop volunteered. "And we were just about to plan the wedding. Y'all wanna be bridesmaids? 'Cause I already got the maid of honor spot."

"Oule, I would love to be in Gem's wedding," Kamani said, a little too excited. "I'm sure it would be real fly."

Immediately I rolled my eyes. I couldn't stand phony chicks.

"What's the problem, Gem?" Kamani said. "You always have an attitude."

"Excuse you? I don't always have an attitude," I snapped.

"I just don't like chicks who pretend. Just be who you are and I'm cool."

"Look, I didn't come over here for a problem. As a matter of fact, I came over here to say congratulations for making the team."

"See?" I hunched my shoulders. "Phony. You tried to play me when I tried out for the team and now that I made it you wanna be all up on me. Girl, bye." I waved my hand dismissively.

"You know what, Gem?" Kamani popped her lips.

"No, I don't know *what*," I said fully charged. "But I do know that *what* will get its behind beat if it comes crazy. So watch *what* you're about to say."

Kamani sighed. "What is your problem? And keep it real. How come you're always getting smart with me? Like everything I say to you is a problem."

"Because that's what it is. A problem. You always got my name in your mouth and I'm tired of it."

"You know what, I'ma just stop trying to be nice to you."

Whoa, what did she say? Rewind. Was she serious or just crazy? *She* was trying to be nice to *me*. Like fa'real dawg, have we been watching the same movie? "Kamani, you can't be serious." It took everything in me not to laugh in her face.

"I'm sooo serious. I even mentioned it to Pop and she said that I should talk to you. So wassup?"

I looked over at Pop. "Yeah, I told her that," Pop said. "But I also told her that you two get smart with each other and that both of y'all needed to drop it. And especially now that we're teammates."

"Pop has a point," Janay said. " 'Cause teamwork makes the dream work."

"Oh wow," I said with my lips twisted. "You searched high and low for that Disney commercial didn't you."

"Gem," Pop said. "Now that wasn't right. Janay didn't do anything to you."

"Whatever."

"See, it's not all them," Pop insisted.

I sucked my teeth. "Okay, whatever."

"I'm really not looking for beef," Kamani said. "We all have the same vision, which is to win. But we need to get along to do that."

"Exactly," Pop said.

I took a deep breath. "Look, I don't have anything against anybody unless they come for me. And truthfully, Kamani, I felt like ever since we met at the twins' party, that you've been comin' for me. Hard. And every time you see me, it's one smart comment after another and another. And I'm not the one."

"Well, I feel the same way," Kamani said. "And I'm really not the one for drama—"

"What? You're the definition of drama," I snapped.

"I could say the same thing about you," Kamani said.

"Say it, but just be ready to deal with the conse-quences," I spat. "And you can believe that."

Kamani popped her eyes. "Let me tell you something, Gem—"

"Would you two just stop it!" Pop said. "Come on. Just drop it and move on. Okay? The party was just a big mis-understanding and now we've moved on from that. We're teammates. The 'Bout-it-Bout-it' crew. And we just need to all get along and be friends. Period."

Kamani didn't say a word and neither did I. Especially since from where I sat Kamani was always—and I do mean always—bringing beef and trying to slaughter me.

"Gem," Kamani sighed. "Look, let's just squash it and start over. Are you cool with that?"

Silence. I tapped the balls of my stilettos. I really wasn't used to making up like this. Usually if somebody constantly aimed for me I cut them off. Period. No second chances. No conversation. Simply finished and vowed to never speak another word to them again. But I guess... maybe...I needed to try something different. I looked over at Pop and her eyes pleaded with me to give it a try.

"All right, Kamani," I said. "Let's start over."

"Straight," she said.

"Okay, so my name is Gem and you are?"

"Kamani," she chuckled. "I've heard a lot about you, Gem."

"Really?"

"Yup. Like how you're a great player who just made the b-ball team. That's wassup."

"Thanks."

"So, I was thinking that like my girl Pop said, you should be a part of our crew."

"And what crew is that?"

"The Rich Girlz."

I paused. I started to remind her that I created the crew, but then I quickly changed my mind and just rolled with it. "That would be kinda hot. I would like that," I said.

"Great." Kamani smiled. "So okay." She looked at Pop and Janay. "Who wants to swear her in?"

"I'll do it." Pop stood up and said, "Stand up, Gem, and place your right hand over your heart."

I complied.

"Now repeat after me," she continued on. "I, Gem."

"I, Gem."

"Accept the honor to be a Rich Girl."

"Accept the honor to be a Rich Girl."

"And I understand—"

"I understand—"

"That being a Rich Girl means—"

"Four things," I took over the pledge. "R stands fa'real fly at all times. I stands for independent of bull. We don't bring it but we will handle it." I snapped my fingers. "C stands for cute. 'Cause that's what we are. And H stands for hot is how we do it."

"And our sole rule." Pop snaked her neck.

"No boyz allowed to come between our crew," I said. "Ever."

Everybody smiled and we sealed the deal with making hearts with our hands and saying our catcall, "Meow."

19

Nothing had ever been so sweet in my life—not my favorite candy, ice cream, chocolate chip cookies (which I was semi-addicted to), not my favorite pair of stilettos, Nikes, or even the crowd roaring after my best jump shot—nothing had ever, ever, ever-ever been as sweet as being Mrs. Ny'eem Parker.

It was electric.

Exciting.

Fantastic.

Fulfilling.

Simply put: it was all dat...and more.

Fa' real.

Ny'eem and I had been together for two months, two weeks, and three days, and every day was better than the last. Never did I expect my life to unfold like this. Ms. Grier said that Ny'eem reminded her of Mr. Khalil and that he was the type of dude that any girl would be happy to have and believe you me, I was.

We were at Ny'eem's spot, which I called the messy bat cave. It was a small studio in downtown Newark, with a sunken area for his bed, red brick walls, wood floors, and exposed ductwork. I was surprised that he could afford a place like this, but he told me that his sister gave him the apartment as a gift, and all he had to do was go to school, work, play ball, and pay the household bills.

Ny'eem lay across the foot of his king-sized bed, with his math book in his hand, while I leaned against his side reading Shakespeare's *Twelfth Night*. Which I totally didn't want to read, but being that I had a test coming up, and had to maintain a B-or-better grade point average to secure my spot on the basketball team—which was on a winning streak by the way—I had to keep my grades up or be chained to the bench; and I was definitely not about the benched life.

"Ny'eem," I said, as his phone rang.

"Wassup?" he said, never once reaching for his phone.

"Are you gon' get that?"

"No."

"Why not?"

" 'Cause I'm here with you and that's more important at the moment. Now wassup?"

I folded the corner of my book's page and then closed it. "I'm hungry."

"Hungry?" He closed his math book. "Yo, what you think, I'm 'spose to feed you 'cause I love you? Nah, you got this baller messed up. I mean you're welcome to eat some cereal. But I'm not about to cook."

Immediately my mind hit rewind and then it went on pause. Did he just tell me that he loved me? Really?

"What did you say?"

"I said you had me messed up," he teased. "Especially, if you think I'ma cook you something to eat. 'Cause I don't do that."

"I'm not talking about cooking. You know exactly what I'm talking about."

He blushed. I couldn't believe my baby blushed for me.... *He really loves me....*

"What?" he said. "What you wanna talk about? If I really just said that I loved you? Yeah I said it and in English, too," he joked.

"Oh, my goodness, poo." Tears of joy filled my eyes. "You really love me," I whined. "Me love you too, poo."

Ny'eem turned over and sat with his back against his black leather headboard. He stared at me, hard, deep, with a million thoughts racing through his eyes.

"What are you thinking about?" I asked him.

"I'm wondering where'd you come from. It's like one day I was hustling solo—going to school, work, kickin' it with my boys here and there, playing ball, and coming home. And that was it. I mean I kicked it with a few shorties but nothing serious and then you showed up."

I slid my arms around his neck and straddled his lap. "And then what happened after I showed up?"

"I fell in love." He gave me a soft peck. "You're funny, you're serious when I need you to be. You tell me about myself if I need to be checked. You're my dude for real. My pot'nah. So yeah, I love you. I love the hell outta you."

I pressed my forehead against his and softly spoke against his lips. "I have never met anyone like you. Ever. And sometimes I wonder if this is a joke and someone is going to come along and say, 'Psych, Gem, this isn't your life.' But this is my life. This *is* my life and I'm thankful that you're in it."

I slipped my tongue into his heated mouth and allowed it to get lost there. He cupped my hips and we kissed, like never before. This kiss was something different.

It had a different feel.

A different magnetism.

A different destination.

Its own zone.

A zone I'd never traveled to before, but wanted to go... needed to go...and needed to go with Ny'eem. Right now. At this moment.

His hands caressed my back and left goose bumps in the trail of his fingertips. His heated touch melted my skin as he lifted my shirt above my head with one hand and reached for the wrapped condom on his nightstand with the other. "You want me to stop?" he whispered as he kissed me along my collarbone.

"No," I whispered back, surrendering to his kisses....

20

"I have a confession," Pop said as me, Kamani, and Janay were in the locker room changing into our uniforms and preparing for practice.

"What's that?" I said as I slipped my shorts on.

Pop took a deep breath. "I want my boo back." She slammed her locker shut. "I can't make him sweat anymore. 'Cause now I'm sweatin' and other than on the court I don't do perspiration."

Silence. I didn't dare open my mouth. Pop and G-Bread was not the convo that I wanted to be involved in.

"Girl, please," Kamani said. "There you go giving in to G-Bread."

"Well, it has been almost three months," Janay said as she laced up her sneakers. "And three months is hella long. He could've married a whole other chick by now and had some kids."

Kamani sucked her teeth. "Janay, stop exaggerating. It's long enough to have another chick, but a kid? Be for real."

"Oule whee, what a great 'Make-me-feel-better-committee.'"
Pop snaked her neck and snapped her fingers. "Imagining
my man with another chick just gave me the urge to cut
somebody."

Don't ask me why but I took two steps back. "Why are
you always so violent?" I frowned at Pop. "You need to get
some help for that."

"I'm not always violent. I just can't imagine G-Bread
with anybody but me."

I looked at Pop and thought, *Girl, he doesn't have another chick. Trust. You are the only one he loves and who
loves his broke butt.*

"That's the problem," Kamani said. "G-Bread knows
that and he takes advantage. You need to make him sweat
for like a year."

"A year?!" Pop and Janay screeched.

"She could be dead by then!" Janay spat. "That's way
too long."

*Ooob-kaaay, now I understood why Janay didn't talk
that much because the ish that came out of her mouth
was ummm...yeah, stooopid.*

"Suppose he does have another chick? Then what?" Kamani asked Pop. "Then how are you going to deal with
that?"

Pop tapped the ball of her left sneaker. "I would be
cool," she said, pacing from one end of the locker room to
the next. "I would be calm." She stopped pacing and
turned toward us. "And I'd be collected. I wouldn't be
mad *at all*. I would just walk right up to the girl and say to
her, 'Looka here boo-boo. See that dude right there, if you
don't leave him alone, I'ma rock you into a sleep that you

won't wake up from.' And then I'ma smile at her and let her know that I'm serious, but I'm still a lady."

I looked at Pop and shook my head. *Out. Of. Control.* Hoping they didn't drag me into telling Man-Man's business, I said, "Okay, I'll meet y'all in the gym."

"Oh hold up, wait a minute," Pop said. "Popcorn's 'bout to put some push up in it. Why didn't I think of this before my head started spinning? Gem, you're his sister and my bff, and since we don't keep secrets, 'cause ain't no boyz allowed to come between us—brothers included—then why don't you tell me if G-Bread is seeing somebody else."

I bit the corner of my lip. Getting in between Pop and Man-Man was not the move. I took a deep breath and for a moment I started to just spit it out and tell Pop about the conversation Man-Man and I had a while back. But I knew a simple run-through of what he'd said to me would never be good enough for Pop. She'd want to know the time he started talking, did he cry, and how many breaths he took before admitting that he missed her. *So nah, I'll just cancel the thought of getting into their business.* "Pop," I said, shaking my head. "Don't put me in the middle of this. If you want Man-Man, I mean G-Bread, back then call him up and tell him that you miss him. You never know, maybe he's learned his lesson."

"Well, you're his sister," Janay said. "Has he learned his lesson or is he married to somebody else now?"

"Be real. Just say it," Kamani insisted.

I sighed. "Look, y'all know Coach likes us to be early for practice. Let's talk about this later."

"Oh, it's like that, Gem?" Pop said, pouring the guilt on extra thick. "It's okay, I understand if you see me suffering and in pain behind G-Bread and, just because he's your brother, and I'm nothing more than your best friend, that you would leave me hanging. It's cool." She sniffed. "I got you. I showed up at your house three ninjas and an ex-con deep to handle some lady, but you can't help me and my heart out. It's cool though, homie. I see how it is."

I huffed. Rolled my eyes to the ceiling. Sucked my teeth. "Look, he misses you, too, okay?"

Pop's face lit up. "When did he tell you that?"

"About two months ago."

"Two months ago?" She twisted her lips. "That's it, two months ago and just once. What kinda missing me is that?"

"Pop," I said. "He's told me that he's missed you every day since then. I told him to tell you that, but he said that he's texted you, called you, tweeted you and the whole nine and you've been ignoring him."

She smiled. "Well how did he say he missed me? Did he say, 'Imissher'? All in one breath? Because if he said it like that, then he just wants to get busy—which ain't gon' happen. Or did he say, 'I miss my baby. I love that girl. She's my world and I can't live without her. I don't ever-ever-ever-ever want to live without her. Matter fact I'ma need a noose if she doesn't come back.' Did he say it like that? 'Cause if he did, then that means he's on the verge of a nervous breakdown and he loves me."

I blinked not once, but four times. "He said all of that *and* more. All you have to do is call him, and he will tell you that he loves you and wants you back. And believe me after you call and tell him that, he will be all over the house borrowing money from everybody to take you out. Trust me on that."

Pop smiled from ear to ear. "My baby still loves me."

"Awwwl, why don't you text him now, before practice starts," Janay said. "That's what I did when me and David broke up. I texted him, his mama, and his step-daddy every day before practice until David saw the error of his ways and begged me back."

I didn't even know what to think of that, so I acted as if Janay didn't just admit that she was a stalker, and said, "We need to get to the gym."

"We have a few more minutes," Pop contended. "And besides, y'all have to help me come up with a plan—Rich Girl Style—to get my man back."

"All you have to do is call him, Pop," I said.

"Yeah, call him," Janay agreed. "And you better call him now, 'cause if you wait until tonight he might jump off a bridge or join the army or something."

Pop looked at Janay like she had two heads. "Janay, you're my girl and all, but you need to start thinking before you speak."

Seriously.

"And Gem, I can't just call him, it's gotta be something bigger than that. Something more romantic like a movie scene or from a romance novel. A story where I can tell my kids how their daddy swept me off my feet."

This chick here . . . is trippin'.

"I got it!" Pop snapped her fingers. "We gon' do a group date. And Gem you make sure that G-Bread is there. We'll meet at Chickey D's on Bloomfield Ave."

"Chickey D's?" I said. "Didn't the health department close that place down?"

"They cleaned it up and it's reopened now," Pop snapped. "And plus they have pizza for five dollars."

"So you want us to go to Chickey D's for five dollar pizza, so that you can get G-Bread back, when you can save us all some money and just call him," I said as I shook my head. "Speechless."

"She doesn't want him to think she's desperate," Kamani said.

"He won't think that," I said. "Just call him."

"And plus," Kamani continued, "Chickey D's is romantic. 'Cause that's where Crook took me for our anniversary."

"What? Stop the press," I said to Kamani. "Your boyfriend's name is Crook?"

"Yeah." She smiled, showing all of her teeth. "That's my baby."

"Well, I don't think I'll be going to eat with anybody that calls themselves Crook," I said.

"And why not?" Kamani said with a slight snap in her tone.

"'Cause I'm just getting my life right. I don't need any problems. And anybody named Crook is on somebody's wanted list, and my new mama don't play that. She is not the one."

"Gem," Pop said adding her two cents in, "Crook is a cool dude. I remember when they first met."

"And it's been on poppin' ever since," Kamani said. "So I don't appreciate you talking about his name, Gem. This is why I don't bring him around my friends and we just chill solo."

"My fault, Kamani," I said. "The name Crook is just a little, well, different."

"Well," she said, "they call him Crook because when he's on the court and the other team has the ball he steals it every time."

"Oh, he plays ball, too?"

"Yes, he does." She rolled her eyes.

"Like I said. My fault," I said. "I shouldn't have said all that. Don't chill solo with your boo, let's all get together and have some fun."

"Bam, exactly." Pop smiled. "Let's have some fun while me and my baby get back together again."

"All right," Kamani said. "So we'll be there."

"Straight," I said. "So Pop, when do you wanna do this? Next week?"

"Next week!" Pop screeched. "It's Friday, oh no, this is an emergency. We need to do this after school. Today. 'Cause by six o'clock I need to be back to boo-lovin'. Hard."

"Today? Then I won't be able to go," Janay said.

"Why not?" Pop looked upset.

"'Cause David has choir rehearsal and I have to be there to watch him."

"Watch him for what? You can't sing," Pop said, frowning.

"Well somebody has to be there to make sure all he does is sing and leave. The last time I left him at choir rehearsal alone, he ran off with the pastor's daughter. So I'm not taking any chances. None."

I really wanted this chick to return to being the quiet Janay. "It's okay, Janay," I said. "We'll hold it down."

"Then today it is." Kamani smiled.

"Yep," Pop said. "Tomorrow it's on!"

"What's on is the clock!" Coach pushed the door open and yelled into the locker room. "And if you ladies don't get in the gym right by the time I count to three, you will spend the next game riding the bench. One...Two..."

21

Since I no longer caught a ride to school with Man-Man and instead caught the bus home with Pop, I wasn't able to catch up with him until I got home this afternoon. I wasn't exactly sure how to tell him that today was the day he needed to beg Pop's forgiveness, because she expected to be boo-lovin' by tonight. But seeing as though we were due to be at Chickey D's in less than an hour I had to tell him something—and quick.

I caught a glimpse of him standing in front of his mirror and splashing cologne along his collar.

I know he's not about to go somewhere.

He slid his black leather jacket on.

Oh...heck...no...I can't deal with Pop if this doesn't jump off.

I pushed open Man-Man's bedroom door and said, "Where are you going?"

He looked at me like I'd lost my mind. "Yo, don't you know to never push a grown man's bedroom door open? You might run up on me runnin' into somethin'."

"Ill. I did not need that visual."

"Well then knock first. Now what you want?" He ran his hands over his goatee.

"I wanna know where you're going?"

"Out. 'Bout to go chill."

"When? Right now?"

"You got it."

"You need to reschedule those plans. I need you to go with me and Ny'eem."

"Lil Sis, please. No offense, but the last time I hung out with Ny'eem all he talked about was you. Messed. Me. Up. So nah, I'll pass, y'all can get that. I got a date anyway." He brushed the waves in his hair.

"A date?! What about Pop?"

"Pop's lost her mind; because anybody that can stay away from me this long it's something wrong with 'em. And besides I'm tired of her ignoring me and not return-ing any of my calls. So I'm done sweatin' her and now I'm back to the days of spreading my playboy love around."

"Now is not the time for that."

"Yes it is. Yesterday I got two friend requests on Face-book from these two chicks. Twins. And you know I got a thing for multiples. They told me they'd been watching my profile and drooling over me. And when I told 'em that they were too fly for me to choose just one, they agreed to let me take 'em both out."

"All three of y'all are going out together? On the same date?" I frowned.

"You got it. That's called helping the economy out. This way instead of having to borrow ten dollars from Toi I just hit her off for five."

"Speechless."

He winked his eye. "A real cat daddy seems to have that effect on people." He popped his invisible collar. "That's why I changed my name from G-Bread, to G-Bread-Pimpin'-Ain't-Dead." He slid his wallet into his back pocket.

While I was too busy being stunned to say anything, Man-Man said, "Dope ain't it?" He shot me a two-finger peace sign and said, "Deuces."

Shaking off my surprise I said, "Wait!"

"I can't. I gotta catch up with these shorties at Chickey D's."

My eyes bugged. "Chickey D's? You can't go there!"

"Girl, please, the food is nasty, but I'm not going there to eat. But in case the twins want something, Chickey D's has five dollar pizzas and I'm broke. Didn't I just tell you that I had to borrow this money from Toi?" He shook his pocket and for a moment it sounded as if he had a collection of silverware rattling in it.

"What is that?"

"It's five dollars worth of quarters. I think Toi was trying to be funny. But hey, money is money. I take dimes and nickels, too."

SMH...I have no idea what Pop sees in him.... "Man-Man, listen, Pop wants to make up with you. So she arranged this group date for all us to hang out at Chickey D's this afternoon. And I have to make sure you're there with flowers in one hand and an apology in the other."

"Did you say this afternoon at Chickey D's?"

"Yes."

"Pop wants to make up with me?"

"Yes. Right now."

"Today?" he asked again.

"Didn't I just answer that?! So you can't go on that date with those two chicks, 'cause Pop will kill 'em."

Man-Man smiled. "That's exactly why I have to go on that date with two chicks. Get Pop all riled up and right when she's about to cut one of 'em, I confess my love to her."

"If you do that, she may not get back with you. She's tired of the games and I know she arranged this crazy date, but still, she just wants you to take her seriously. That's it. So that's why she left you alone for almost three months to teach you a lesson. And if you go in there playing games, she may never speak to you again. Do you want that?"

Man-Man stood silent for a moment and then he said, "I do miss her." He sat down on the edge of his bed. "That's my girl for real. No other girl compares to Pop. Not one."

"Then cancel that date with the ghetto-ghetto twins so that you can come with me and Ny'eem and tell Pop how you feel."

"But what if I get there and she's changed her mind or not feeling me again?"

"G-Bread-Pimpin'-Ain't-Dead, believe me, you don't have to worry about that."

"A'ight." He reached for his cell phone. "Let me call the twins and cancel my date with them." He dialed a number, paused, and then said, "Aye, yo, is this Twin Number One or Number Two?" Pause. "Number One, a'ight well this is Prince Nazeem from Brick City."

Prince who?

"And I won't be able to make it tonight. I'm trying to get

back with my girl. But I'ma forward your friend request to my lil brother, Baby-Tot-Tot. He can practice kicking it to chicks on y'all. You know I gotta keep the love in the family...Hello...hello?" Man-Man looked over at me. "Guess they got mad 'cause they couldn't have me. Oh well." He hunched his shoulders. "Let's roll."

I'll be hiding out in the bathroom, **Pop's text read**. And I'ma stay there 'til y'all arrive. So text me when you get here, so I can make a grand entrance.

K, I replied.

I was in the car with my baby, Ny'eem, and Man-Man followed behind us in his own ride. "Who's meeting us here again?" Ny'eem asked.

"My crew," I said. "And why do you keep asking me that?"

" 'Cause I can't understand why y'all would choose Chickey D's. They serve heart attacks on the menu."

"Okay, Mr. Fitness, could you chill? Like wassup with you? Why do you seem on edge this afternoon?"

He took a deep breath. "We lost our game yesterday."

"Awwl. My baby's a sore loser? Next time I'll make sure I'm there to be your good luck charm. As long as I don't have a game on the same day."

Ny'eem smiled. "I'm not a sore loser." He pulled into a parking space. "I'm just a great winner."

"Yeah, I bet you are." I smiled, as I texted Pop, We're here. Wait ten minutes and then getcha abracadabra on.

Ny'eem walked around the car and opened my door. "This is probably the only place in America that sells pepperoni-flavored pork chops as a pizza topping."

"Whatever." I cracked up. "They don't sell pepperoni-flavored pork chops."

"They may as well," Man-Man said walking up behind us and giving Ny'eem a fist bump. " 'Cause the last time I was here the food made me so sick, I thought for sure I ate a stroke."

"Fa' real?" I asked, as we walked in.

"Fa' sho, good thing I started praying. I was like, yo God, I'm 'spose to kick it at the club tonight, Chief."

Ny'eem cracked up and Man-Man said, "You know what I'm sayin?"

Once we walked into the small two-room restaurant the waitress, who also doubled as the cashier, met us at the door, smacking on a pack and half of gum. "Yeah, y'allz dinin' in or takin' er'thing out?"

I blinked, because her southern accent was so thick that for a minute I wondered if we were in the deep woods of Florida somewhere. She looked at me and smiled and of course she had a diamond grill. "Oh, you look real purdy. Whicha lil get-up on."

I didn't know whether to say "thank you" or check this chick for calling my top, leggings, and heels a get-up. I decided to let her slide and say, "Thanks. And we're staying. It's six of us."

She showed us to our table and said, "All right now, make sure y'all leave a tip."

I looked at Man-Man and asked him, "Is that one of the ghetto-ghetto twins?"

Before he could respond my cell phone beeped letting me know I had a text. It was from Pop. Meet me in the bathroom.

I looked at Man-Man and Ny'eem. "I'll be back."

I squeezed my way into the single stalled bathroom where Pop was. She wore a cute black miniskirt with a yellow top and heels. "Awwl, look at you, boo," I said. "You look too cute."

"That's how I do it." She snaked her neck and snapped her fingers.

"So are you ready to make your grand entrance?" I asked her. "Man-Man and Ny'eem are at the table, where's Kamani and her boo? They're running late?"

"Gurl, Kamani's mother be buggin' sometimes. So who knows. She probably told Kamani she couldn't hang out after school, that room needed cleaning or something. And plus you know Kamani has a little sister and brother, so she's the built-in babysitter. She tried to get me to come over to her house once to help her watch her brother and sister and I had to tell her, 'Oh no, boo-boo, I don't like kids.'" She curled her upper lip.

"Pop."

"What? It's the truth."

"Shaking my head at you, Pop."

"Anywho." She ran her hand along the sides of her curves. "We've in been in this tight bathroom long enough. Time to go and get my snucker-boo."

Pop and I switched our way from the bathroom and both Ny'eem and Man-Man looked up and smiled. Man-Man stood up and met Pop halfway. "Let me hollah at you real quick," Man-Man said to Pop, dropping his deep sexy voice on her. One thing about Man-Man was that only his relatives knew underneath that smooth voice and cute looks was a seventeen-year-old, who never cleaned up his room, and borrowed money from his sisters for a living.

I could look at Pop and tell she was formulating a slick way to say no to Man-Man, so he could beg her until she said yes. That's exactly why I took over and said, "Yeah, she can hollah at you real quick." I gave Pop a soft nudge with my shoulder and said, "Go 'head. Mrs. G-Bread-Pimpin'-Ain't-Dead."

Pop smiled, Man-Man took her by the hand, and they walked outside. They were gone for about ten minutes and I'm not sure what they said, but I do know that by the time they walked back in, Man-Man was holding Pop's waist and she was grinnin' super-hard.

"My favorite couple's back together again?" I clapped my hands. "Awwl, look at them, poo," I said to Ny'eem. "Boo-lovin's back in style."

Pop snaked her neck. "And you know it." Snap. Snap.

Pop and Man-Man slid into the booth with me and Ny'eem. They sat directly across from us.

"Ny'eem," I said. "This is my bestie, Pop. And Pop, this is my boyfriend, Ny'eem." I caressed his hand.

"Wassup, Pop," Ny'eem said, draping his arm over my shoulder. "I've heard a lot about you."

"Hey…" Pop hesitated, and then she paused and looked at Ny'eem with a blank stare. After what seemed like at least ten seconds she blinked. "You know what, I have to go to the bathroom." She looked at Man-Man. "I'll be right back, sweetie." She looked over at me. "Don't you have to go to the bathroom?"

"No."

"Ahh, yeah you do." She shot Ny'eem a plastic smile and then looked at me with her eyes bucking. "Come on."

Once we were in the bathroom Pop locked the door and I said, "What is wrong with you?"

"Gem..." She paused, then tapped her fingers like an accordion against the side of the small sink. "Umm..." She paused again.

"Would you just say it!" I said aggravated.

"Okay, your lil cutie, Ny'eem looks a lot like Kamani's boo, Crook."

"What?" I said taken aback. "Say that again."

She let out a deep breath. "Gem, I ain't sayin', but I'm just sayin', they look like the same dude." She paused, let what she'd said marinate in the air for a minute, and then she went on. "Unless they're brothers or have the same daddy or something."

I gave a nervous laugh. "Girl, bye. Ny'eem is not even that type of guy. And besides, you've seen Kamani's boyfriend before, right?"

"Right," she agreed.

"Well then you would know if he and Ny'eem were the same person."

She shook her head. "No I wouldn't. I saw Crook twice last year. Early last year. When he first kicked it to Kamani and a week later I ran into them at the bowling alley. But that was the last time I saw him."

"They're not the same person," I said. "Ny'eem doesn't even have a nickname."

"I hope not." She sighed and then quickly snapped her fingers. "I got it! This is what I'll do. When we get back to the table I'ma tell him that he looks real familiar and I'ma ask him if they call him Crook. If he says, 'no,' then we'll eat, chill with our cuties, and be happy. But, if he says, 'yeah,' then you gon' play it cool. And I'ma say I have an emergency at home and we need to go. Game?"

"Game."

We walked back to the table and my stomach felt like it was filled with sick butterflies. Ny'eem looked directly in my eyes as I slid into the booth next to him. "You a'ight?" he asked me.

"Yeah, I'm cool." I nervously grabbed a menu and combed through it.

He stared at me a little longer than I wanted him to. For a moment I felt like he could read my mind.

"So umm, Ny'eem," Pop called for his attention. "You look soooo familiar to me. You're from Newark, right?"

"Yeah," he said, looking at me out the corner of his eyes. "Born and raised."

"Okay." Pop looked at the menu. "I think I want pep-peroni pizza."

"Sounds good to me," Man-Man said.

"So umm, Ny'eem," Pop said. "Do you have a street name? By chance do they call you Crook?"

"Yeah," he squinted. "How'd you know that?"

"Small world I guess. How'd you get a name like that?"

"Because of how I play ball. 'Cause whenever the op-posing team has it, I steal it."

Pop looked over at me and her eyes clearly said, "Yeah this is the same dude."

My heart dropped to my feet and immediately tears beat against the back of my eyes.

Don't cry…Don't cry…Don't cry…Don't cry…

"You know what?" Pop said as she scrolled through her

cell phone. "I have an emergency and I need to get home right away."

"Oh, you have an emergency?" I managed to say.

"Okay, I'll take you home, Pop," Man-Man volunteered.

"No," Pop snapped a little harder than she should've. "It's fine. Me and Gem will catch the bus." She looked at me. "Let's go." And we scurried out of the restaurant before Ny'eem or Man-Man could stop us.

22

Pop and I rode the bus in silence. I'm not sure if we were quiet because she knew that I would cry at any moment, so she decided not to say much—or she didn't exactly know what to say. She'd texted Kamani and told her that we were on our way over to her house for an emergency meeting. And she'd texted Janay and told her that David's choir rehearsal needed to go on standby, because my life, once again, was in shambles.

"The good thing," Pop said, as I bit into my bottom lip and looked out the window, "is that Kamani only lives around the corner from me, so if we feel the urge to go and mess up Ny'eem, Benny is only a couch and cell phone minutes away."

I didn't respond, I was too busy wondering how I could be so stupid.

Ny'eem must've called me a thousand times and each time I sent him to voice mail.

Seriously, what was I going to say to him? How could

you play me? How could you do me this way? What did I do to deserve this? There was no way I could ask him any of those questions. Not when I felt like I'd asked those same freakin' questions all of my life.

I'd asked them since my mother used to hide in the bathroom all day and night and get high. Since I realized that I didn't know my father because my mother didn't know who he was. Since I was placed in foster care and my mother never came and got me. All of my life I'd asked those questions and I was tired of it.

So eff it.

It was what it was. And if I'd rolled with everything else that had come my way, then I could roll with the most recent gut punch—that my boyfriend—who I loved so much and thought was so great—was nothing more than... nothing.

Tears clouded my eyes and as fast as they fell I wiped them away. Pop placed her arm over my shoulder and said, "If you want, I'll break up with G-Bread and then we can both share in this misery."

"Nah, I'm good," I said, feeling numb.

Pop pressed the buzzer and signaled the driver to let us off at the next stop.

We walked quietly up the block and to the apartment complex Kamani lived in. We pressed Kamani's bell and before anyone answered Pop said, "Gem, you're not in this alone. We're girls. All of us. And we're not gon' let some buster come between our crew. So the Rich Girlz got you, trust."

"Thanks, Pop," I said. But there was nothing she could say that wouldn't make me feel alone. Because I was alone.

Kamani buzzed us in. We caught the elevator to her third-floor apartment. The door was open and Kamani's little sister showed us to Kamani's room, where she and Janay were parked on the bed and sending out tweets.

Pop and I sat on the edge of Kamani's bed and Janay said, "This better be good, because although the pastor's daughter was gone, I did leave David there with the first lady."

"Would you please," Pop said, agitated. "No one wants to hear about Eddie Long, I mean David and his church-capades, okay. Now moving on to some serious ish." She looked at Kamani. "We got a problem."

"What, it's ninja time?" Kamani asked.

"No, it's way worse than that," Pop said.

"So what is it?"

"You know we went to Chickey D's after school—"

"Oh yeah," Kamani interrupted. "I couldn't make it. Crook told me that he had basketball practice to go to."

Pop rolled her eyes to the ceiling. "He is such a liar, Kamani. He didn't have basketball practice."

"How do you know that?"

"Because he was sitting up there at Chickey D's with Gem."

"What?!" Kamani screeched. "What do you mean? What are you saying?"

"I'm saying that your boyfriend, Crook, is Gem's boyfriend, Ny'eem."

Kamani laughed and waved her hand. "Girl, please. Gem could never pull Crook."

"And what the hell does that mean?" I looked at Kamani all crazy.

"I'm just saying that Crook is so into me, that other chicks don't even exist to him."

Pop frowned. "They don't exist when you're around, but when you're gone there's some serious hocus-pocus going on. And you can believe that."

"Well I *don't* believe that," Kamani said.

I stared at Kamani and I wondered if underneath it all we shared the same pain or was she truly in denial.

"But Pop and Gem," Janay added her half a cent in. "Why would you two think that Crook and Ny'eem would be the same person when those are two different names? Obviously they're two different people."

Pop looked at Janay as if she could've slapped her.

"Crook is his street name," I managed to say, without too much tremble in my voice. "Ny'eem is his real name. And when Pop asked him why they called him Crook he said it was because of the way he plays ball."

"He said that?" Kamani bit the inside of her cheek. "He told you this?"

"Yeah."

"My Crook?" she said in disbelief. "My Crook who has his own spot?"

"Yeah, the spot that his sister, Elite the R&B singer, bought him," I said.

"He looks like Wale? With a sleeve of tattoos? Dark skin—"

"Yeah, damn!" I snapped. "It's the same guy!" Tears filled my eyes. "What part don't you understand! He's been playing us! And that's the problem." Tears rolled down my cheeks.

"What you crying for?!" Kamani screamed.

"'Cause I loved him and he hurt me! I'm tired of being played!" Unwanted tears rolled down my face. "Damn!" I hated this. Crying was such a weakness.

"I can't believe you're standing here crying over my man!" Kamani spat.

"Your man," Pop snapped. "He's been both of y'all man, that's the problem!"

"Oh, hell no!" Kamani said. "He hasn't been both of our man, because I've been with him for over a year, so I've been the main chick, don't get it messed up—"

"We can't possibly get it any more messed up than what you got it," Pop said pissed. "Are you slippin' or forgettin' that no boy is supposed to come between our clique?"

"No I didn't forget. That's why I'm looking at Gem crazy. As much as I talk about Crook you're really trying to tell me you didn't know that he was my man. Girl, please. I don't believe that. You've been smiling in my face and doing me dirty behind my back!" Kamani raised up off of the bed and pointed into my face. Which instantly caused all of us to stand up, and divide into unspoken teams. Janay stood next to Kamani and me and Pop stood together.

"I don't know what you gang-bangin' at the mouth for," I said to Kamani. "But where I come from if you raise up that means you're about to bring it. And I ain't never been afraid to buck, so wassup? 'Cause I'm trying to explain to you that we both got played. I didn't go after your man. I didn't even know what your boyfriend's name was until at practice today. So what you sound to me—is ridiculous!"

"And you sound like a skank whore!" Kamani spat. "You must've gave him some, 'cause anybody from the streets is easy. But one thing I ain't scared of and that I know for sure is that I'm not gon' let some homeless, ratchet-crackhead foster kid take my man from me. Period. So my advice to you, Rich Girl, is to fall back or get dealt with. So step off!"

"Wait, wait, wait," Pop interrupted. "This is going too far—"

"No it hasn't." I took two steps toward Kamani. " 'Cause I'ma take it a little farther. Be clear, I don't do threats. I just smack the crap outta you until you get some sense. And if you keep coming at me crazy, I will be forced to give you the slap that all stupid chicks need. Now my advice to you, Rich Girl, is to calm down 'cause if you keep talkin', this ratchet-crackhead foster kid will lay you down. And I'm from the streets, so I don't fight fair, I make sure lungs collapse. So hear me on this, I'ma step-off and not because I'm afraid of you, but because I don't do no-good dudes. But since you do, he's all yours."

"I don't believe you, Kamani," Pop said. "You gon' bug over some dude who doesn't even have enough respect for you to be faithful?!"

"At least he's not breaking up with me every other day, like G-Bread is doing you." Kamani rolled her eyes. "So you're the last one to talk."

"You better keep G-Bread's name outcha mouth!" Pop spat.

"Look," I said, feeling as if I was due to break at any minute. "I'm done, 'cause I don't argue with chickens. Are you ready, Pop?"

"Yeah, I'm ready to pop!" Pop spat. "I don't believe this," she said as we stormed out of Kamani's apartment and slammed the door behind us. I didn't open my mouth or look at Pop until I'd reached my house and made it to my room. And then, as if a swift wind had come by and kicked me in the stomach and something had gripped me in the chest, I leaned against the wall, slid to the floor and cried for what felt like forever.

23

"Aye, yo, what you doing?"
I didn't have to look up to know that was Man-Man standing in my doorway. With the exception of the street-lamp's glow that spilled in through my mini-blind slats, my room was a misty black until Man-Man walked in and the light from the hallway spilled onto my carpeted floor, where I'd been sitting for hours. My knees were pulled to my chest and my head was held down.

Since I'd been sitting here I did manage to get up once, so that I could convince Pop I was okay enough for her to leave. Even though I wasn't. I just wanted to cry in peace—without hearing, "It'll be okay. It'll be all right." I really didn't want to be soothed and I definitely didn't want to be lied to. I knew Pop meant well, but we both knew that nothing would ever be okay again. Not with the way I felt—as if someone had gripped my throat and left their fist there.

I sniffed and wiped my eyes and although I didn't hold my head up, I did manage to turn to the side, look at Man-Man, and say, "I'm just sitting here. I'm okay."

"You're sitting on your floor in the dark and you're okay? Yeah a'ight, you already know you can keep it real with me." Man-Man closed my door and slid onto the floor next to me. "Pop told me what happened."

The fist clutched around my throat made it hard to swallow but, I did, and then I asked Man-Man, "Did you know...about her?" Silent tears ran down my cheeks and Man-Man took one of his sleeves and wiped them away.

"Nah, I didn't know. I had no idea. And if I did, I would've deaded the whole deal from the beginning. There's no way I would've let him be with my little sister."

I felt my chest preparing to explode...five...four..."I thought he was so different." Three...two... "And all he did was play me..." One...! I broke into tears that felt like they'd come from the bottom of my feet. I did my best to control my internal explosion—but I felt like I'd lost my mind. Like I was really going crazy.

Insane.

I felt like I was spinning...and I didn't want to spin. I wanted the day that I met Ny'eem back, the first day he kicked it to me back, the first time we kissed back, the day I gave my virginity to him back, I wanted it all back so that I could take it and spit on it. Because none of it was worth me feeling like I had a bullet lodged in my chest.

"Awl man," Man-Man sighed. "Yo, don't cry." He draped his arm around me and pulled me to his chest. "Don't cry, lil sis." He stroked my hair. "I don't believe this," he said, more to himself than to me. After a few minutes of me having a crying convulsion Man-Man said, "I don't know if it'll make you feel better or not, but I called Crook and I let him know that the next time I saw him I was gon' see about him. 'Cause ain't no way he can rock with me or be my boy and he hurt you like this. Nah, I'ma slaughter 'im, for real, son."

I wanted to tell Man-Man to just leave Crook alone, because I knew that telling Man-Man to drop it was the right thing to say, but truth be told, I wanted somebody to take Crook and two-piece him. I just didn't know if it needed to be my brother.

"Gem!" Ms. Grier yelled and simultaneously opened my door. "Ny'eem...is...here..." She paused and flicked the light on. "What's going on in here?" She looked down at me. "You've been crying? What are you crying for? Did somebody do something to you?" she asked me, not coming up for air. "Somebody hurt you? Cousin Shake!" she yelled, not giving me a chance to answer any of her million and one questions. "I think we might need to call up Aunt Nona's son, Shy-Pookie, is he out of jail yet?"

"Nawl!" Cousin Shake yelled back. "Remember he was on the news last week for holding up that grocery store? Well, they had a ten thousand dollar reward for anybody who could help lead to his arrest, and I turned him in. Me and Minnie'll be in Hawaii next week. Why?" he asked, filling my doorway. He paused as he looked down at us. "Man-Man, why are you all hugged up on your lil sister? Don't you know insectory is illegal?"

"It's incest," Ms. Grier corrected him. "And he was comforting her. She's crying and won't tell me why."

"Because you won't be quiet long enough for her to answer you, Ma," Man-Man snapped.

Ms. Grier gave him a warning eye and said, "Somebody needs to tell me what the problem is. And right now."

"It's Ny'eem," Man-Man answered. "He did some real foul stuff. Which is why I'm about to go downstairs and handle him."

"No!" I hopped up off the floor. "Don't! Let me go and talk to him, please."

"Nah—"

"Man-Man. I need to do this."

He hesitated. "A'ight, but he got one time to come out the side of his neck and I'ma floor him."

"Awl, hell," Cousin Shake said. "Let me go and get my yo-azz-better-be-cool stick."

I walked down the stairs and although my family didn't follow directly behind me, I could feel them watching me. Ny'eem stood in the center of the living room and his eyes looked worried. Sad. Confused.

I walked over to him and he said, "You got a minute?"

"Not really." I bit my bottom lip.

Don't cry...don't cry...you better not cry in front of him...

I swallowed and said, "So make it quick."

"Can we get a little privacy?"

"No!" Ms. Grier yelled down the stairs.

"Why you always so nice, Grier?!" Cousin Shake snapped, slapping a duct taped bat in the palm of his right hand. "Hell no, you can't get no privacy! Apparently you been a lil too private, that's the problem!"

"I'll be okay." I turned around toward the stairs and looked at them standing there. "I'ma just step outside for a minute."

I didn't wait for them to protest. Instead, I walked quickly onto the porch and Ny'eem was behind me.

"What?" I spat.

Ny'eem reached for my hands and I snatched them back. "Oh, it's like that? You don't even want me touching you?" he said.

"Never again." I twisted my lips.

"Gem, listen to me." He walked up close to me and I took two steps back. He stopped in his tracks and said, "Do you know how much I love you? I would never cheat on you."

"You didn't cheat on me," I spat. "You cheated with me. Kamani was the main chick."

"What?" He looked disgusted. "I don't even know who you or your brother are talking about—"

I rolled my eyes to the sky. "Don't you think you've lied enough? Now you don't know the girl? Can't you come better than that?"

"It's the truth!"

"It's a lie and you know it!" I shook my head. "I'm soooo stupid. Here I thought you really loved me—"

"I do love you!"

"I thought you were soooo real. Like one of the best things that ever happened to me. I thought you were different—"

"I am different!"

"You're nothing!" I spat. "If anything you're a lying dog. That's why you would never answer your phone when I was around. And why you've been acting so funny toward me—"

"I didn't answer my phone because I knew whoever

was calling me wasn't as important as you. And I haven't been acting funny toward you—"

"You were acting funny this afternoon. It wasn't about you losing a game, it was about your main girl wanting to be with you."

"The only girl I have is you!"

"You don't have me. I'm not your girl!"

"What?" Ny'eem hesitated. "So you really gon' let some bird come along and dead all that we have."

"We don't have nothing but a buncha lies. Here I thought that my life couldn't possibly get any better than finally having a family and a boyfriend that I loved. Do you know how much I trusted you? Do you know how I felt when that girl told me she was your girl and that you were her man? I felt like nothing. Like nothing." I pushed him in his chest and tears slipped from my eyes. I turned toward the door to go back inside and Ny'eem grabbed me by my forearm and spun me back around toward him.

"Gem, I need you to believe me and understand that I didn't cheat on you. I love you. I swear I love you more than anybody I've ever loved. You make my life complete. Believe me."

"How can I believe anything you say, and you won't even admit that you know the chick?"

"I don't!"

"Oh so, you really don't know Kamani Sanders, but Kamani Sanders knows you like the back of her hand and swears you're her man!"

Ny'eem paused and then he said, "I kicked it to her for a minute—"

The fist that had gripped my throat had now moved and was beating me in the back of my head, but instead of crumbling and giving in to the pain I chuckled in disbelief and said, "First you don't know her. And now you kicked it to her for a minute. Whatever. We're done. Through. It's over and I don't ever want to see you again! I hate you!"

"Oh word," he said calmly, but his eyes welled with tears. "So you just gon' bounce? Like what we had is nothing."

He paused and I stood silently, doing all I could to stop the tears that were revealing too many of my feelings.

"That's what you're saying, right?" he pushed.

"Yeah," I swallowed, still looking away from him. "Exactly."

Ny'eem softly turned my face toward his and said, "Keep it gutter with me in my face. Now say it, since you loved me yesterday and hate me today. Look me in my eyes and tell me that. Say it. Because I promise you if you say it and you mean it then I'll step all the way off. But, if you can't say it, then that means you don't mean it. Which means we gon' fix this because I didn't do anything!"

I looked Ny'eem in his eyes and when I realized that tears were seriously threatening to spill from them, there was no way I could tell him that I hated him, because I didn't. I loved him and that's what I hated. "Ny'eem," I sighed. "It's over. I'm done."

"Nah," he said and took a step back. "This is far from over, and I put that on everything I love."

24

"Time to get up." Ms. Grier walked into my room, pulled the curtains back and opened the blinds. "It's been two days. The whole house has given you space and now it's time to get things back in order. Now sit up." She tapped the edge of my bed. "Come on. Sit up."

Just when I thought she wasn't crazy anymore...

I slid the covers from over my head and the sunlight she'd let into my room blinded me. I quickly squeezed my eyes shut, took a deep breath, and slowly peeled them open, one at a time.

"Sit up," she said, sitting on the edge of my bed. "I want to talk to you."

I sniffed and hoped that when I sat up—that this time, unlike yesterday and the day before that, that I could sit up without unwanted tears sneaking up on me and spilling down my cheeks.

I was tired of crying.

Tired of being weak.

And yeah, I'd had a broken heart before, but the difference between those and this one—this time I felt like my heart was killing me.

And I didn't want to die. I wanted to act like none of this existed.

But it existed. And every waking minute reminded me of it...

I thought when I cut up all of Ny'eem's pictures that the pain would go away. But it didn't—it just left a mess. A mess that I sailed and scattered across the room and now everywhere I looked there he was, literally.

And then there were the memories, etched in my head like mind tattoos.

I felt paralyzed.

I couldn't eat.

Couldn't sleep.

Couldn't even dream in peace.

All I could do was think about Ny'eem and replay Kamani telling me that he was her man...her man...not mine...

"Come on, I said sit up," Ms. Grier repeated. She gently pulled the covers down and over my shoulders. I looked up at her and tears filled my eyes.

"Oh, baby," she said, hugging me. "It's okay—"

I hate that phrase... it's anything but okay...

A few minutes after giving in to these stupid tears I wiped my eyes and sat up. My hair spilled wildly over my shoulders and not until I sat up did I realize that I was wearing one of Ny'eem's basketball T-shirts that he'd given me. I fought off the urge to break down again and instead crossed my legs Indian style, "I'm up," I said to Ms. Grier.

She stroked my hair behind my ears and smiled at me. It was clearly a sympathetic smile. "I know it's hard and I know it hurts."

Don't cry again... I thought to myself, as my lips started to tremble.

"And I know," she continued, "that you may not think or believe that things will get better, but they will."

"I want them to get better now," I managed to say and then I threw in a nervous laugh. "Right now."

"It's no magic pill to heal, baby."

"I just loved him so much," I said without thinking, "and he hurt me. He could've just left me alone or never said anything to me from the beginning. He didn't have to use me. I didn't deserve that. I feel...so stupid."

I held my head down and surrendered to feeling like a fool.

"Let me tell you something," Ms. Grier said sternly. "You are anything but stupid. There is nothing stupid about loving someone and wanting to be with them. There is nothing stupid about being true. Nothing stupid about walking away when they've hurt you. You are not stupid. In life things happen, and love happens, and sometimes love happens over and over again. That's just the way it is sometimes. I was nineteen years old when I gave birth to the twins. I was married to their father for over ten years. I loved him and he loved me, but it didn't work out."

"Why?" I asked.

"Because he made other choices," Ms. Grier said.

"Did he cheat on you?" The look on her face said it all. "So they all cheat," I said as I shook my head.

"That's not what I'm saying," Ms. Grier said. "What I'm

saying is that things happen. And yes, he took me through some things and some of the things I chose to stand there and take. But when I decided to get up and out of the bed and take care of myself is when my life came together."

"I wish it was that easy for me. But he's in all my thoughts. I can't even think about him without crying!"

"Gem, my brown beauty, you are a smart girl and I'm telling you that it's okay to cry for a little while, but it's not okay to cry forever. You don't give your power away to anybody, for anything. And when you are in a relationship and it no longer feels good it's because it's not good anymore. Move on. Love doesn't hurt. Lies do. Deceit hurts."

"But I thought he loved me."

"And he may have loved you, honey, but is that enough when he was manipulative? Love is a beautiful thing, and it has absolutely nothing to do with pain. When it turns into pain, walk away."

"Just like that?"

"At sixteen, yes, you can walk away just like that. You are responsible for the decisions that you make. And as your mother I'm telling you that I'm raising you to be a strong young woman because around here strength is an expectation and that's bottom line."

"I understand that, but still..."

"There are no buts and there is no time to stand still."

"Maybe you're right, maybe being with him was just a mistake." I shrugged, hopelessly.

"In life there are no mistakes, only lessons—"

"And what lesson is this? That I have a bottomless well of tears?"

"The lesson is strength. The lesson is you are beautiful no matter what your circumstances are. Now I want you

out of this bed, dressed, and back to handling your business." She stroked my cheek. "I'm serious."

"Okay." I gave her a small smile.

"Now you go on and get ready for school. Your father
and I have a parent-teacher conference for your brother
Malik that we have to get to. Seems he's trying to be the
class clown."

25

After practice I was torn about whether to shower and change in the locker room or if I should've waited until I got home. I'd rather deal with Cousin Shake's tirade about me smelling up the living room and putting a bad taste in his food than deal with the tension and the ra-ra that I knew awaited me in the locker room.

Not that I was scared.

I just didn't feel like squashing rumors, cussing Janay out, and gripping Kamani by the roots of her sew-in and dragging her through the shower stalls.

It just wasn't worth the three-game suspension—not when I was getting more playtime than she was. Not when I was scoring more points in a single game than she had ever scored. And not when I knew that if I dragged her I'd beat her so bad that the three-game suspension would probably turn out to be a jail sentence.

But, I didn't want to look like the punk either.

So, I figured to heck with it, if anybody came for me, I'd

just have to show 'em why stepping out of bounds wasn't a good idea. Pop had already told me that she was down for whatever; and if she saw me toss a swing that she'd follow up with an uppercut first and worry about what happened when we got to the police station.

"Umm hmm, she was trying to do me dirty and be a home wrecker," Kamani said to her captivated and signifying crowd. "But like my man, Crook, told me, it's always gon' be gutter-rat-groupies trying to come between us." All the girls standing around Kamani created a choir of 'that's a mess, girl' and one of them even said, "I knew she was a trick." Yet, when Pop and I stood in their faces, instead of behind their backs, all of the random chatter ceased. Some of the girls even left the locker room altogether.

"I thought so," Pop said loudly. "They don't want none!"

And I guess they didn't, because no one said a word as we walked into our individual shower stalls.

I showered quickly because I just wanted to get out of there. Everybody stared at me, talked about me, was all in my business—and no matter how many girls I could tackle to the ground and sling by their hair it wouldn't stop the pain that fly-kicked me in the chest.

So, I needed to get home, because I knew that at any moment tears would knock against the back of my eyes again.

Pop and I stepped out of the shower, got dressed, and then walked over to the lounge area, where Kamani continued on with her rant. "Yeah, me and Crook spent last night together. He was so scared of losing me that I had to stay with him to prove that I was ride or die." She turned around, rolled her eyes at me, and continued, "And I proved—all night—how ride or die I was. I wouldn't be surprised if he's back at my door tonight again, begging for a repeat."

Don't say anything, let it go.

I can't let her play me…

I swallowed the iron fist in my throat, smiled at Pop, and said, "Are you ready?"

"Yop," said Pop, who definitely was not smiling. "I'm ready for a few things."

"Girl, we don't sweat the small stuff." I waved my hand and looked over at Kamani—who was staring at me. I bucked my eyes at her and said, "Any particular reason why you're looking dead in my mouth? You wouldn't be worried would you?"

"Worried?" She arched a brow.

"That I'ma take your man again, 'cause I can assure you, boo-boo, that I've already got what I needed and I'm now finished with him. You can have him back."

The look on Kamani's face told me I'd sent her straight to twenty. But I didn't give a damn, 'cause honestly, I was looking for a reason to leave her with some lumps.

I cocked my neck to the side and mouthed to Kamani, "Bring it. I dare you."

Before she could get up the muscle or the nerve Janay skipped in smacking on a lollipop and said, "Kamaneee, your boo's outside. He wanna talk to you."

Pause… What? What did Janay say? Ny'eem is here? Really? Ny'eem is actually here for Kamani? He is really her man… really, really, her man… I don't know what I did to piss God off, but obviously for this to be happening, Jesus has beef with me.

I swallowed.

Did my best to maintain my game face.

Pop turned fire red. "I'ma beat his—"

"Pop, just drop it. It's cool," I said, determined to keep my composure, 'cause there was no way I would let any of these chicks see me sweat.

Not. Even. An Option.

Kamani looked nervous as she said to Janay, "Crook's outside for me?"

"Where else would he be, Kamani," Janay giggled. "He can't walk through walls. And he said hurry up."

Kamani blushed. "Told y'all." She looked from one end of the room to the next. "That's my baby." She turned toward Janay. "How do I look?"

"Cute," Janay said. "Real cute. Just put a lil gloss on."

"Okay." Kamani searched through her purse, pulled out her gloss and shined her lips. "How does my gloss look, Nicole?" she said to one of the girls on the team, who'd been mesmerized by Kamani's rants about Crook. "Are they poppin', girl?"

Nicole smiled and said, "They're poppin', girl. You look real cute. Now go on and get your hottie." She snapped her fingers. " 'Cause you already know everybody's trying to get up on 'im."

"Maybe I should go freshen up first," Kamani said.

"Kamani," Janay said. "You just took a shower, so you got an hour before you start sweating and everything. And anyway boo-boo seemed a little agitated when he asked for you. So I wouldn't keep him waiting."

"And plus I wanna meet him," Nicole said.

"Me too," said a few of the other girls from the team.

I wanted to run out of there, but there was no way I could do that. So I just stood there and wondered was this even real? Or was this a nightmare...but then, nightmares didn't last this long.

I looked at Pop and she whispered to me, "All you have to do is say the word, and I will have my cousin Benny over here shuttin' down the block. As long as you have twenty dollars for his cell phone minutes, girl he will take over the world."

"No, I'm cool." I slung my duffle bag over my shoulder. "I couldn't care less what Ny'eem, or better yet, Crook does with that hollah-back-thirsty-bird."

"What you say, Gem?" Kamani barked my way.

"I said, that I don't care what Crook-Ny'eem, whatever his name is does with you, you hollah-back-bird."

"You forgot, thirsty—" Pop added.

"Oh, yeah, hollah-back-thirsty-bird."

"You can call me names all day," Kamani said. "But one thing you can't call me is the sideline ho!"

Janay sarcastically clapped her hands and said, "All up in ya grill with the truth! Now come on, Kamani, and go get your man."

"Yeah," Kamani said, "I think I'll do that, jealous trick." She walked out of the locker room and the heavy metal door made a thud sound as it slammed in place.

"What did she say?!" Pop raced toward the door. "Did she call you a jealous trick?"

Before Pop could bolt out after Kamani I said, "Just let it go."

"What?" Pop batted her lashes as if she were returning from another planet. "Let it go, are you serious?"

"Leave it alone. I'm not sweatin' it," I said, struggling to act as if my confidence hadn't been kicked to an all-time low.

Pop blinked. "All right." She paused. "All right. Since this is your fight. I'ma let you direct it, but just know they got one mo' time to say something crazy and it's on!"

We walked out of the locker room and the closer I got to the exit door the heavier my feet felt. I couldn't believe that this was happening to me. There was no way Ny'eem ever loved me. No way.

I approached the glass exit doors and saw Ny'eem standing there. He was dressed in slightly baggy black jeans, a black YMCMB hoodie, and Air Yeezy sneakers. The look on his face said that he was stressed. He locked eyes with me and for a moment I thought maybe he missed me. *Check yourself.*

I shifted my eyes from his and instead made it my business to put a little more swish in my hips as I placed my hand on the handle, pushed the door open, and prepared to walk past him.

"Are you sure you don't want to slap him?" Pop asked me. " 'Cause thugs don't scare me."

"I just want to ignore him," I said, slyly sipping in a nervous breath.

"Kamani," Ny'eem called out to her as she took slow steps toward him. "Come on, ma, what you waiting on? Come here." He smiled at her and she smiled back. She looked over at me and I guess the hurt in my eyes caused her to put pep in her step and switch her way over to Ny'eem. Most of the team stood around and either gawked at Ny'eem or chuckled while taking sneak peeks at me.

"He got any friends, Kamani?" Nicole giggled.

"Yeah, girl," Kamani said. "Plenty." She strolled over to Ny'eem and said, "Wassup, boo?"

"You know exactly wassup." Ny'eem looked over at me, as Pop and I were attempting to walk swiftly away, and said, "Yo, let me hollah at you real quick."

"She doesn't need to come over here!" Kamani snapped.

"I sure don't. 'Cause I don't do threesomes, you and your little freak can leave me out of your mess!" I said to Ny'eem.

"I said come here," Ny'eem said sternly.

"And I said I'm good."

"Gem, don't play with me," he said as the veins in his neck stuck out and made a road map into his shoulders.

"Go 'head," Pop said. " 'Cause this just might be the excuse we need to jump him."

Reluctantly I walked over toward Ny'eem and Pop followed closely behind me. "What?" I said with major attitude. "What you want? Ain't that your girl right here?" I pointed to Kamani. "Haven't you been disrespectful enough?"

Ny'eem looked at Kamani. "You told her I was your man?"

Kamani paused, placed her hands on her hips, and said, "Yeah, because you are."

"Really, Kamani, I'm your man, me?" Ny'eem looked taken aback. "Seriously?" He pointed to his chest.

"I don't have time for this!" I snapped.

"Be quiet," Ny'eem said to me. "You talk too soon and you jump to conclusions too much. So stand there, don't move, and bigger than that don't say a word." He turned back to Kamani and said, "Yo, I don't know what you lyin' for—"

"I'm not lyin'!" she screamed.

"Yo," Ny'eem spat. "You buggin' for real, 'cause me and

you ain't never been nothin'. Ever. And yeah, I kicked it to you for a week, took you bowling, and treated you to a chicken sandwich and a Coke off the dollar menu at Wendy's, but a cheap date doesn't make you my girl. It just makes you a cheap date."

"Why are you doing this, Crook?" Kamani asked. "Why you frontin' like this?"

"Frontin'?" Ny'eem curled his upper lip and pointed his hand like a gun into her face. "Kamani, don't play with me. 'Cause if you were a dude I would've already finished you. Now be clear since it seems you've been lying about this since last year, ya not my girl. Period."

"Whatever!" Kamani said, waving her hand, doing all she could to play off her embarrassment. "I don't know what you trying to pretend for—"

"Yo, I don't know whether you're stupid or crazy, but how about this, I come from the guts of the gutter so you can't get no crazier than me. Which means you got about two seconds to straighten this out or its gon' be a problem, for real, son."

"I don't have to argue with you, Crook," Kamani said. "Whatever."

"It's not whatever. Me and you never existed. Now admit it!" He walked up close to her and stared her down.

"Okay, okay," she said, looking frightened. "Whatever. We're not together. That's fine."

"We were never together." He stepped even closer to her. "I know."

"I thought so." Ny'eem took a step back. "Liar."

Pop snapped, "I don't believe you lied, Kamani! Are you crazy? Why would you do something like that?! I don't believe this! You're lucky Gem doesn't drag you! I don't believe that all this time you've been lying! You went to the bottom of the psycho-sea with that one. The queen of sickness, lying about Crook being your boyfriend. Who does that!"

"Pop you need to mind your business!" Kamani screamed. "And you need to get some business. Real business and not make-believe. Freakin' bipolar schizoid!" Pop turned to me. "Are you ready yet to swing on this chick? 'Cause my fist is itchin'!"

Yeah, I was ready to swing, but I had to get out of shock first. Just as I came to, I said to Kamani, "You are one psychotic beyotch! You seriously need your throat sliced, but honestly, you're not even worth it!"

"Whatever." Kamani flicked her wrist. "I don't gotta stand here for this! Come on, Janay. Let's go!"

Janay looked at Kamani and twisted her lips. She shook her head and said, "Uh ah, I ain't going nowhere with you, hand that rocks the cradle. You have lost your mind. Seems you've watched *Obsessed* one too many times and I'm concerned."

"Oh really. Is that how it is?" Kamani asked in disbelief. "Nicole, come on."

"Chile, please," Nicole said. "Do you, 'cause I'm done."

"Jade, Briana." Kamani looked around and called a few of the girls who were standing there.

"Kamani, puhlease," Jade said. "You have never said anything to us a day in your life. So don't try and call on us because you don't have any friends."

"To hell with y'all then!"

"Girl, please," Janay said. "Go hop on that lil bus and ride off into the sunset, psycho. That is not your man and we are not your friends. That kinda crazy has to be contagious and I don't know where you got it from, but I don't want you giving it to me."

"Whatever." Kamani choked back tears, still trying to play tough. She ran across the street and immediately hopped on the bus that came her way. All the girls waved bye as she rode away.

"Oules" and "Oh, my Gods" filled the air and the crowd standing around went into a frantic buzz.

I still hadn't said anything to Ny'eem, but I knew I needed to say something.

But what?

I was a mix between embarrassed, relieved, and in disbelief and I didn't know how to express that—or if I should've expressed that...

Say something. I looked at Ny'eem and said, "Umm, I just want to say to you—"

"Oh, now you have something to say to me?" he snapped. "Nah, you hate me, remember?"

"I don't hate you," I said. "I was just—"

"Being ridiculous. Because it was easier for you to believe some sick-lyin' chick than it was for you to believe me."

"I didn't know what to think—"

"Oh really, your thoughts seemed real clear to me. You let somebody get you hyped up and then instead of talking to me, you wanted me to step. Bounce. Because somewhere in all that we shared, you forgot that I was a real dude who loved you."

"Ny'eem, would you just let me explain?"

"Did you let me explain?" He took two steps back.

"So you just gon' walk away?" I took two steps forward.

"Isn't that what you did?"

I stopped in my tracks, and when I didn't answer, he said, "Yeah, that's exactly what you did." Ny'eem turned and left me center stage with my heart pounding. This was worse than crying for days. I didn't know which way to turn or what to do. All I knew was that I loved him too much not to go after him. But I couldn't move. And not because I didn't want to, but because for a moment I felt undeserving of everything turning out to be so perfect. Could this really be my life? Did I actually have a chance to have everything? A family, a boyfriend...friends....

Me. A motherless kid who never had anybody...could I turn out to have the whole world? This was soooo crazy. Maybe I didn't deserve all of this. Maybe I needed to let him walk away.

I swallowed. I felt the fear of being a failure and of not ever having anything creep up on me. I didn't know what to do, but suddenly I knew that watching my fairy tale cross the street while I stood here and opted to punish myself was stupid.

"What are you waiting on?" Pop said to me. "Gem." She nudged my shoulder. "Are you really going to just let him leave like that?"

I hesitated. "Maybe, maybe it's meant to be this way. If it's too good to be true then—"

"Look," she snapped. "I don't know what you're standing here going through, but that's your boo, Cinderella. Now, you better go and handle your scandal before it gets to driving down Springfield Avenue."

"You think I'm buggin'...maybe...a little?"

"No, I don't think that. I think you're buggin' a whole hellava lot!"

I paused. Pop was right. I was more than buggin'. I was about to turn toward the dark side and go crazy. I had to bring it back fast and I had to go and get my man. I ran across the street.

"Ny'eem, listen to me." I grabbed him by his arm and he turned toward me. "I know I messed up. But I just always—"

"Expect the worst."

I swallowed, did my best to hold back tears. "Yeah. I keep telling myself that this is not too good to be real, but every now and then I get scared. I shouldn't have believed Kamani. I should've talked to you. I should've. And I'm sorry. I am." Tears slid down my cheeks. "But know this— I love you and I want to be with you. And I will never ever believe some b.s. that some psycho bird tells me about you."

He stared at me for what felt like forever. "I missed you."

I crowded his personal space and slid my arms around his neck. "I missed you, too."

"Don't ever do anything like that again."

I nodded. "Never again."

I pressed my forehead against the base of his neck and said, "I love you."

Surrendering, Ny'eem placed his hands on my waist, lifted me in the air so that we were face-to-face, and whispered against my lips. "I know you do, and I love you, too."

NO BOYZ ALLOWED

Ni-Ni Simone

ABOUT THIS GUIDE

The following questions are intended to
enhance your group's reading of
NO BOYZ ALLOWED.

Discussion Questions

1. What did you think of Gem's attitude when she arrived at her new foster home? Do you think she had a right to be angry or should she have dropped the attitude?

2. What did you think of Malik's reaction to Gem when she said she didn't want to stay in their new foster home? Do you think he should've agreed with Gem simply because she was his sister?

3. What did you think would happen to Gem when she ran away? Do you think running away ever solves problems?

4. What did you think of Gem's birth mother? Do you know someone who has a mother like Gem's?

5. How did you feel about Gem being a foster child? Do you know any foster children? Do they act like Gem? If you were a foster child, would you act like Gem? Do you think there are any good foster homes?

6. When do you think Gem started to change and become more comfortable with her foster family?

7. What did you think of Gem's relationship with Man-Man? Were you surprised that he treated her like family from the beginning?

8. What did you think of Gem's friends?

9. In what way do you feel Ny'eem changed Gem's life?

10. If you were to rewrite this story, how would you change it?

COMING SOON!

Hollywood High

by Ni-Ni Simone and Amir Abrams

Welcome to Hollywood High, where socialites rule and popularity is more of a drug than designer digs could ever be.

1

London

Listen up and weep. Let me tell you what sets me apart
from the rest of these wannabe-fabulous broads.

I *am* fabulous.

From the beauty mole on the upper-left side of my
pouty, seductive lips to my high cheekbones and big,
brown sultry eyes, I'm that milk-chocolate dipped beauty
with the slim waist, long sculpted legs, and triple-stacked
booty that had all the cuties wishing their girl could be
me. And somewhere in this world, there was a nation of
gorilla-faced hood rats paying the price for all of this gor-
geousness. *Boom,* thought you knew! Born in London—
hint, hint. Cultured in Paris, and molded in New York, the
big city of dreams. And now living here in La-La Land—the
capital of fakes, flakes, and multiple plastic surgeries. Oh…
and a bunch of smog!

Pampered, honey-waxed, and glowing from the UMO
24-karat gold facial I just had an hour ago, it was only right
that I did what a diva does best—be diva-licious, of course.

So, I slowly pulled up to the entrance of Hollywood High, exactly three minutes and fifty-four seconds before the bell rang, in my brand-new customized chocolate brown Aston Martin Vantage Roadster with the hot pink interior. I had to have every upgrade possible to make sure I stayed two steps ahead of the rest of these West Coast hoes. By the time I was done, Daddy dropped a check for over a hundred-and-sixty grand. Please, that's how we do it. Write checks first, ask questions later. I had to bring it! Had to serve it! Especially since I heard that Rich—Hollywood High's princess of ghetto fabulousness— would be rolling up in the most expensive car on the planet.

Ghetto bird or not, I really couldn't hate on her. Three reasons: a) her father had the whole music industry on lock with his record label; b) she was West Coast royalty; and c) my daddy, Turner Phillips, Esquire, was her father's attorney. So there you have it. Oh, but don't get it twisted. From litigation to contract negotiations, with law offices in London, Beverly Hills, and New York, Daddy was the power-house go-to-attorney for all the entertainment elite across the globe. So my budding friendship with Rich was not just out of a long history of business dealings between my Daddy and hers, but out of necessity.

Image was everything here. Who you knew and what you owned and where you lived all defined you. So sur-rounding myself with the Who's Who of Hollywood was the only way to do it, boo. And right now, Rich, Spencer, and Heather—like it or not—were Hollywood's "It Girls." And the minute I stepped through those glass doors, I was about to become the newest member.

Heads turned as I rolled up to valet with the world in the palm of my paraffin-smooth hands, blaring Nicki Minaj's

"Moment 4 Life" out of my Bang & Olufsen BeoSound stereo. I needed to make sure that everyone saw my personalized tags: LONDON. Yep, that's me! London Phillips— fine, fly and forever fabulous. Oh, and did I mention... drop dead gorgeous? That's right. My moment to shine happened the day I was born. And the limelight had shone on me ever since. From magazine ads and television commercials to the catwalks of Milan and Rome, I may have been new to Hollywood High, but I was *not* new to the world of glitz and glamour, or the clicking of flash bulbs in my face.

Grab a pad and pen. And take notes. I was taking the fashion world by storm and being groomed by the best in the industry long before any of these Hollywood hoes knew what Dior, Chanel, or Yves St. Laurent stood for: class, style, and sophistication. And none of these bitches could serve me, okay. Not when I had an international supermodel for a mother, who kept me laced in all of the hottest wears (or as they say in France, *haute couture*) from Paris and Milan.

For those who don't know: yes, supermodel Jade Phillips was my mother. With her jet black hair and exotic features, she'd graced the covers of *Vogue*, *Marie Claire*, *L'Officiel*— a high-end fashion magazine in France and seventy other countries across the world—and she was also featured in *TIME*'s fashion magazine section for being one of the most sought out models in the industry. And now she'd made it her life's mission to make sure I follow in her diamond-studded footsteps down the catwalk, no matter what. Hence the reason why I forced myself to drink down that god-awful seaweed smoothie, compliments of yet another one of her ridiculous diet plans to rid me of my dangerous curves so that I'd be runway ready, as she liked to call it. Translation: a protruding collarbone, flat chest, narrow hips, and a pancake-flat behind—a walking campaign ad for Feed the Hungry. *Ugh!*

I flipped down my visor to check my face and hair to make sure everything was in place, then stepped out of my car, leaving the door open and the engine running for the valet attendant. I handed him my pink canister filled with my mother's green gook. "Here. Toss this mess, then clean out my cup." He gave me a shocked look, clearly not used to being given orders. But he would learn today. "Umm, did I stutter?"

"No, ma'am."

"Good. And I want my car washed and waxed by three."

"Yes, ma'am. Welcome to Hollywood High."

"Whatever." I shook my naturally thick and wavy hair from side to side, pulled my Chanels down over my eyes to block the sparkling sun and the ungodly sight of a group of Chia Pets standing around gawking. Yeah, I knew they saw my work. Two-carat pink diamond studs bling-blinging in my ears. Pink Hermès Birkin bag draped in the crook of my arm, six-inch Louis Vuitton stilettos on my feet, as I stood with poise. Back straight. Hip forward. One foot in front of the other. Always ready for a photo shoot. Lights! Camera! High Fashion! Should I give you my autograph now or later? *Click, click!*

2

Rich

The scarlet-red bottoms of my six-inch Louboutins gleamed as the butterfly doors of my hot pink Bugatti inched into the air and I stepped out and into the spotlight of the California sun. The heated rays washed over me as I sashayed down the red carpet and toward the all-glass student entrance. I was minutes shy of the morning bell, of course.

Voilá, grand entrance.

An all-eyes-on-the-princess type of thing. Rewind that. Now replace princess with sixteen-year-old queen.

Yes, I was doin' it. Poppin' it in the press, rockin' it on all the blogs, and my face alone—no matter the headline—glamorized even the cheapest tabloid.

And yeah, I was an attention whore. And yeah, umm hmm, it was a dirty job. Scandalous. But somebody had to have it on lock.

Amen?

Amen.

Besides, starring in the media was an inherited jewel that came with being international royalty. Daughter of the legendary billionaire, hip-hop artist, and groundbreaking record executive, once known as M.C. Wickedness and now solely known as Richard G. Montgomery Sr., President and C.E.O. of the renowned Grand Records.

Think hotter than Jay-Z.

Signed more talent than Clive Davis.

More platinum records than Lady Gaga or her monsters could ever dream.

Think big, strong, strapping, chocolate, and handsome and you've got my daddy.

And yes, I'm a daddy's girl.

But bigger than that, I'm the exact design and manifestation of my mother's plan to get rich or die trying—hailing from the gutters of Watts, a cramped two-bedroom, concrete ranch, with black bars on the windows and a single palm tree in the front yard—to a sixty-two thousand square foot, fully staffed, and electronically gated, sixty acre piece of 90210 paradise. Needless to say, my mother did the damn thing.

And yeah, once upon a time she was a groupie, but so what? We should all aspire to be upgraded. From dating the local hood rich thugs, to swooning her way into the hottest clubs, becoming a staple backstage at all the concerts, to finally clicking her Cinderella heels into the right place at the right time—my daddy's dressing room—and the rest is married-with-two-kids-and-smiling-all-the-way-to the-bank history.

And sure, there was a prenup, but again, so what? Like my mother, the one and only Logan Montgomery, said, giving birth to my brother and me let my daddy know it was cheaper to keep her.

Cha-ching!

So, with parents like mine my life added up to this: my social status was better and bigger than the porno-tape that made Kim Trick-dashian relevant and hotter than the ex-con Paris Hilton's jail scandal. I was flyer than Beyoncé and wealthier than Blue Ivy. From the moment I was born, I had fans, wannabes, and frenemies secretly praying to God that they'd wake up and be me. Because along with being royalty I was the epitome of beauty: radiant chestnut skin, sparkling marble brown eyes, lashes that extended and curled perfectly at the ends, and a 5' 6", brick house thick body that every chick in L.A. would tango with death and sell their last breath to the plastic surgeon to get.

Yeah, it was like that. Trust. My voluptuous milkshake owned the yard.

And it's not that my shit didn't stink, it's just that my daddy had a PR team to ensure the scent faded away quickly.

Believe me, my biggest concern was my Parisian stylist making sure that I murdered the fashion scene.

I refreshed the pink gloss on my full lips and took a quick peek at my reflection in the mirrored entrance door. My blunt Chinese bob lay flush against my sharp jawline and swung with just the right bounce as I confirmed that my glowing eye shadow and blush was Barbie-doll perfect and complemented my catwalk-ready ensemble. Black diamond studded hoops, fitted red skinny leg jeans, a navy short-sleeve blazer with a Burberry crest on the right breast pocket, a blue and white striped camisole, four strands of sixty-inch pearls, and a signature Gucci tote dangled around my wrist.

A wide smile crept upon me.

Crèmedelacrème.com.

I stepped across the glass threshold and teens of all shapes and sizes lined the marble hallways and hung out in front of their mahogany lockers. There were a few newbies—better known as new-money—who stared at me and were in straight fan mode. I blessed them with a small fan of the fingers and then I continued on my way. I had zero interest in newbies, especially since I knew that by this time next year, most of them would be broke and back in public school throwing up gang signs. Okay!

Soooo, moving right along.

I swayed my hips and worked the catwalk toward my locker, and just as I was about to break into a Naomi Campbell freeze, pose, and turn, for no other reason than being fabulous, the words, "Hi, Rich!" slapped me in the face and almost caused me to stumble.

What the...

I steadied my balance and blinked, not once but four times. It was Spencer, my ex-ex-ex-years ago-ex-bff, like first grade bff—who I only spoke to and continued to claim because she was good for my image and my mother made me do it.

And, yeah, I guess I'll admit I kind of liked her—sometimes—like one or two days out of the year, maybe. But every other day this chick worked my nerves. Why? Because she was el stupido, dumb, and loco all rolled up into one.

I lifted my eyes to the ceiling, slowly rolled them back down, and then hit her with a smile. "Hey, girlfriend."

"Hiiiiii." She gave me a tight smile and clenched her teeth.

Gag me.

I hit her with a Miss America wave and double-cheeked air kisses.

I guess that wasn't enough for her, because instead of rolling with the moment, this chick snatched a hug from me and I almost hurled. Ev'ver'ree. Where.

Spencer released me and I stood stunned. She carried on, "It's so great to see you! I just got back from the French Alps in Spain." She paused. Tapped her temple with her manicured index finger. "Or was that San Francisco? But anyway, I couldn't wait to get back to Hollywood High! I can't believe we're back in school already!"

I couldn't speak. I couldn't. And I didn't know what shocked me more: that she put her hands on me, or that she smelled like the perfume aisle at Walgreens.

OMG, my eyes are burning...

"Are you okay, Rich?"

Did she attack me?

I blinked.

Say something...

I blinked again.

Did I die...?

Say. Something.

"Umm, girl, yeah," I said, coming to and pinching myself to confirm that I was still alive. "What are you wearing? You smell—"

"Delish?" She completed my sentence. "It's La-Voom, Heather's mother's new scent. She asked me to try it and being that I'm nice like that, I did." She spun around as if she were modeling new clothes. "You like?" She batted her button eyes.

Hell no. "I think it's fantast!" I cleared my throat. "But do tell, is she still secretly selling her line out of a storage shed? Or did the courts settle that class action lawsuit against her for that terrible skin rash she caused people?"

Spencer hesitated. "Skin rash?"

"Skin to the rash. And I really hope she's seen the error of her...ways...." My voice drifted. "Oh my...wow." I looked Spencer over, and my eyes blinked rapidly. "Dam'yum!" I said tight-lipped. "Have you been wandering Skid Row and doing homeless boys again—?"

"Homeless boys—?" She placed her hands on her hips.

"Don't act as if you've never been on the creep-creep with a busted boo and his cardboard box."

"How dare you!" Spencer's eyes narrowed.

"What did I do?!" I pointed at the bumpy alien on her neck. "I'm trying to help you and bring that nastiness to your attention. And if you haven't been entertaining busters, then Heather's mother did it to you!"

"Did it to me?" Spencer's eyes bugged and her neck swerved. "I don't go that way! And for your information, I have never wandered Skid Row. I knew exactly where I was going! And I didn't know Joey was homeless. He lied and told me that cardboard box was a science experiment. How dare you bring that up! I'm not some low-level hoochie. So get your zig-zag straight. Because I know you don't want me to talk about your secret visit in a blond wig to an STD clinic. Fire crotch. Queen of the itch, itch."

My chocolate skin turned flaming red, and the South Central in my genes was two seconds from waking up and doing a drive-by sling. I swallowed, drank in two deep breaths, and reloaded with an exhale. "Listen here, Bubbles, do you have Botox leaking from your lips or something? Certainly you already know talking nasty to me is not an option, because I will take my Gucci-covered wrist and beat you into a smart moment. I'm sooo not the one! So I advise you to back up." I pointed my finger into her face and squinted. "All the way up."

"You better—"

"The only commitment I have to the word better, is that I *better* stay rich and I *better* stay beautiful, anything other than that is optional. Now you on the other hand—what you *better* do is shut your mouth, take your compact out, and look at the pimple face bearrilla growing on your neck!"

She gasped.

And I waited for something else nasty to slip from her lips. I'd had enough. Over. It. Besides, my mother taught me that talking only went thus far, and when you tired of the chatter, you were to slant your neck and click-click-boom your hater with a threat that their dirtiest little secret was an e-mail away from being on tabloid blast. "Now, Spencer," I batted my lashes and said with a tinge of concern, "I'm hoping your silence means you've discovered that all of this ying-yang is not the move for you. So, may I suggest that you shut the hell up? Unless, of course, you want the world to uncover that freaky blue videotaped secret you and your mother hope like hell the Vatican will pray away."

All the color left her face and her lips clapped shut.

I smiled and mouthed, "Pow! Now hit the floor with that."

3

Spencer

I can't stand Rich! That bug-eyed beetle walked around here like she was Queen It when all she really was, was cheap and easy, ready to give it up at the first hello. Trampette should've been her first name, and ManEater her last. I should've pulled out my crystal nail file and slapped her big face with it. Who did she think she was?

I fanned my hand out over the front of my denim mini-dress, shifting the weight of my one-hundred-and-eighteen-pound frame from one six-inch, pink-heeled foot to the other. Unlike Rich, who was one beef patty short of a Whopper, I was dancer-toned and could wear anything and look fabulous in it. But I *chose* not to be over-the-top with it because unlike Rich and everyone else here at Holly-wood High, *I* didn't have to impress anyone. I was natu-rally beautiful and knew it.

And yeah, she was cute and all. And, yeah, she dressed like no other. But Trampette forgot I knew who she was *before* Jenny Craig and *before* she had those bunched-up teeth shaved down and straightened out. I knew her when she was a chunky bucktooth Teletubby running around and losing her breath on the playground. So there was no way Miss Chipmunk wanted to roll down in the gutter with me 'cause I was the Ace of Spades when it came to messy!

I shook my shoulder-length curls out of my face, pulled out my compact, and then smacked my Chanel-glossed lips. I wanted to die but I couldn't let pie-face know that, so I said, "Umm, Rich, how about *you* shut *your* mouth. After all the morning-after pills you've popped in the last two years, I can't believe you'd stand here and wanna piss in my Crunch Berries. Oh, no Miss Plan B, *you* had better seal your own doors shut, *first*, before you start tryna walk through mine. You're the reason they invented Plan B in the first place."

I turned my neck from side to side and blinked my hazel eyes. *Sweet…merciful…kumquats!* Heather's mother's perfume had chewed my neck up. I wanted to scream!

Rich spat, "You wouldn't be trying to get anything crunked would you, Ditsy Doodle? You—"

"OhmyGod," London interrupted our argument. Her heels screeched against the floor as she said, "Here you are!" She air-kissed Rich, then eyed me, slowly.

Oh, no, this hot-buttered beeswax snooty-booty didn't!

London continued, "I've been wandering around this monstrous place all morning…" She paused and twisted her perfectly painted lips. "What's that smell?" London frowned and waved her hand under her nose, and sniffed. "Is that, is that you, Spencer?"

"Umm hmm," Rich said. "She's wearing La-Voom, from the freak-nasty-rash collection. Doesn't it smell delish?"

"No. That mess stinks. It smells like cat piss."

Rich laughed. "Girrrrl, I didn't wanna be the one to say it, since Ms. Thang wears her feelings like a diamond bangle, but since you took it there, *meeeeeeeeow!*"

The two of them cackled like two messy sea hens. Wait, hens aren't in the sea, right? No, of course not. Well, that's what they sounded like. So that's what they were.

"I can't believe you'd say that?!" I spat, snapping my compact shut, stuffing it back into my Louis Vuitton Tribute bag.

"Whaaaaatever," London said, waving me on like I was some second-class trash. "Do you, boo. And while you're at it. You might want to invest in some Valtrex for those nasty bumps around your neck."

I frowned. "*Valtrex?* Are you serious? For what?"

She snapped her fingers in my face. "Uh, helllllllo, Space Cadet. For that nastiness around your neck, what else? It looks like a bad case of herpes, boo."

Rich snickered.

I inhaled. Exhaled.

Batted my lashes.

Looks like I'm going to have to serve her, too.

I swept a curl away from my face and tucked it behind my ear.

Counted to ten in my head. 'Cause in five…four… three…two…one, I was about to set it up—wait, wait, I meant set it off—up in this mother suckey-duckey, okay? I mean. It was one thing for Rich to try it. After all, we've *known* each other since my mother—media giant and bil-

lionaire Kitty Ellington, the famed TV producer and host
of her internationally popular talk show, *Dish the Dirt*—
along with Rich's dad, insisted we become friends for
image's sake. And in the capital of plastics, appearance
was everything. So I put up with Rich's foolery because I
had to.

But, that chicken-foot broad London, who I only met
over the summer through Rich, needed a reality check—
and *quick*, before I brought the rain down on her. Newsflash: I might not have been as braggadocious as the two
of them phonies, but I came from just as much money as
Rich's daddy and definitely more than London's family
would ever have. So she had better back that thang-a-lang
up on a grill 'cause I was seconds from frying her goose.
"You know what, London, you better watch your panty
liner!"

She wrinkled her nose and put a finger up. "Pause."

Did she just put her finger in my face?

"Pump, pump, pump it back," I snapped, shifting my
handbag from one hand to the other, putting a hand up
on my hip. My gold and diamond bangles clanked. "You
don't *pause* me, Miss Snicker-Doodle-Doo. I'm no CD
player! And before you start with your snot ball comments
get your facts straight, Miss Know It All. I don't own a cat.
I'm allergic to them. So why would I wear cat piss? And I
don't have herpes. Besides, how would I get it around my
neck? It's just a nasty rash from Mrs. Cummings' new perfume. So that goes to show you how much you know. And
they call me confused. Go figure."

"You wait one damn minute, Dumbo," London hissed.

"Dumbo?!" I'll have you know I have the highest GPA in

this whole entire school." I shot a look over at Rich, who was laughing hysterically. "Unlike some of *you* hyenas who have to buy your grades, *I'm* not the one walking around here with the IQ of a Popsicle."

Rich raised her neatly arched brow.

London clapped her hands. "Good for you. Now…like I was saying, *Dumbo*, I don't know how you dizzy hoes do it here at Hollywood High, but I will floor you girlfriend, okay. Don't do it to yourself."

I frowned, slammed my locker shut. "Oh…my…God! You've gone too far now, London. That may be how *you* hoes in New York do it. But we don't do that kind of perverted nastiness over here on the West Coast."

She frowned. "*Excuse* you?"

I huffed. "I didn't stutter, Miss Nasty. I *said* you went too damn far telling me not to do it to myself, like I go around playing in my goodie box or something."

Rich and London stared at each other, then burst into laughter.

I stomped off just as the homeroom bell rang. My curls bounced wildly as my stilettos jabbed the marbled floor beneath me. *Welcome to Hollywood High,* trick! *The first chance I get, I'm gonna knock Miss London's playhouse down right from underneath her nose.*

But first, I had more pressing issues to think about. I needed to get an emergency dermatologist appointment to handle this itchy, burning rash. My heels scurried as I made a left into the girls' lounge instead of a right into homeroom. I locked myself into the powder room. I had to get out of here!

OMG, there was a wildfire burning around my neck.

Ooooh, when I get back from the doctor's office, I'm gonna jumpstart Heather's caboose for her mother trying to do me in like this.

I dialed 9-1-1.

The operator answered on the first ring, "Operator, what's your emergency?"

Immediately, I screamed, "Camille Cummings, the washed-up drunk, has set my neck on fire!"

4

Heather

My eyes were heavy.
Sinking.

And the more I struggled to keep them open, the heavier they felt. I wasn't sure what time it was. I just knew that dull yellow rays had eased their way through the slits of my electronic blinds, so I guessed it was daylight.

Early morning, maybe?

Maybe...?

My head was splitting.

Pounding.

The room was spinning.

I tried to steady myself in bed, but I couldn't get my neck to hold up my head.

I needed to get it together.

I had something to do.

Think, think, think...what was it...

I don't know.

Damn.

I fell back against my pillow and a few small goose feathers floated into the air like dust mites.

I was messed up. Literally.

My mouth was dry. Chalky. And I could taste the stale Belvedere that had chased my way to space. No, no, it wasn't space. It was Heaven. It had chased my way to the side of Heaven that the crushed up street candy, Black Beauty, always took me to. A place where I loved to be...where I didn't need to snort Adderall to feel better, happier, alive. A place where I was always a star and never had to come off the set of my hit show, or step out of the character I played: Wu-Wu Tanner. The pop-lock-and-droppin'-it fun, loving, exciting, animal-print wearing, suburban teenager with a pain in the butt little sister, an old dog, and parents who loved Wu-Wu and her crazy antics.

A place where I was nothing like myself—Heather Cummings. I was better than Heather. I was Wu-Wu. A star. Every day. All day.

I lay back on my king-sized wrought iron bed and giggled at the thought that I was two crushed pills away from returning to Heaven.

I closed my eyes and just as I envisioned Wu-Wu throwing a wild and crazy neighborhood party, "You better get up!" sliced its way through my thoughts. "And I mean right now!"

I didn't have to open my eyes or turn toward the door to know that was Camille, my mother.

The official high blower.

"I don't know if you think you're Madame Butterfly, Raven-Simoné, or Halle Berry!" she announced as she moseyed her way into my room and her matted mink slippers slapped against the wood floor. "But I can tell you this, the cockamamie bull you're trying to pull this morning—"

So it was morning.

She continued, "Will not work. So if you know what's best for you, you'll get up and make your way to school!"

OMG! That's what I have to do! It's the first day of school.

My eyes popped open and immediately landed on my wall clock: 10:30 A.M. It was already third period.

I sat up and Camille stood at the foot of my bed with her daily uniform on: a long and silky white, spaghetti-strap, see-through nightgown, matted mink slippers, and a drink in her hand—judging from the color it was either brandy or Scotch. I looked into her glassy blue eyes. It was Scotch for sure. She shook her glass and the ice rattled. She flipped her honey blond hair over her blotchy red shoulders and peered at me.

I shook my head. God, I hated that we resembled. I had her thin upper lip, the same small mole on my left eyelid, her high cheekbones, her height: 5' 6", her shape: busty: 34D, narrow hips and small butt.

Our differences: I looked Latin although I wasn't. I was somewhere in between my white mother and mysterious black father. My skin was Mexican bronze, or more like a white girl baked by the Caribbean sun. My hair was Sicilian thick and full of sandy brown coils. My chocolate eyes were shaped like an ancient Egyptian's. Slanted. Set in al-monds. I didn't really look white and I definitely didn't look black. I just looked...different. Biracial—whatever that was. All I knew is that I hated it.

Which is why, up until the age of ten, every year for my birthday I'd always blow out the candles with a wish that I could either look white like my mother or black like my father.

This in-between thing didn't work for me. I didn't want it. And I especially didn't like looking Spanish when I wasn't Spanish. And the worst was when people asked me what was I? Where did I come from? Or someone would instantly speak Spanish to me! WTF! How about I only spoke English! And what was I? I was an American mutt who just wanted to belong somewhere, anywhere other than the lonely and confused middle.

Damn.

"Heather Suzanne Cummings," Camille spat as she rattled her drink and caused some of it to spill over the rim. "I'm asking you not to try me this morning, because I am in no mood. Therefore, I advise you to get up and make your way to school—"

"What, are you running for PTA president or something?" I snapped as I tossed the covers off of me and stood to the floor. "Or is there a parent-teachers' meeting you're finally going to show up to?"

Camille let out a sarcastic laugh and then she stopped abruptly. "Don't be offensive. Now shut it." She sipped her drink and tapped her foot. Her voice slurred a little. "I don't give a damn about those teachers' meetings or PETA, or PTTA, PTA or whatever it is. I care about my career, a career that you owe me."

"I don't owe you anything!" I walked into my closet and she followed behind me.

"You owe me everything!" she screamed. "I know you don't think you're hot because you have your own show, do you?" She snorted. "Well, let me blow your high, missy—"

You already have...

She carried on. "You being the star of that show is only because of me. It's because of me and my career you were even offered the audition. I'm the star! Not you! Not Wu-Wu! But me, Camille Cummings, Oscar award–winning—"

"Drunk!" I spat. "You're the Oscar award–winning and washed-up drunk! Whose career died three failed rehabs and a million bottles ago—!"

WHAP!!!!

Camille's hand crashed against my right cheek and forced my neck to whip to the left and get stuck there.

She downed the rest of her drink and took a step back. For a moment I thought she was preparing to assume a boxer's position. Instead, she squinted her eyes and pointed at me. "If my career died, it's because I slept with the devil and gave birth to you! You ungrateful little witch. Now," she said through clenched teeth as she lowered her brow, "I suggest you get to school, be seen with that snotty nose clique. And if the paparazzi happens to show up, you better mention my name every chance you get!"

"I'm not—"

"You *will*. And *you will* like it. And *you will* be nice to those girls and act as if you like each and every one of them, and especially that fat, pissy, princess Rich!" She reached into her glass, popped a piece of ice into her mouth, and crunched on it. "The driver will be waiting. So hurry up!" She stormed out of my room and slammed the door behind her.

I stood frozen. I couldn't believe that she'd put her hands on me. I started to run out of the room after her, but quickly changed my mind. She wasn't worth chipping a nail, let alone attacking her and giving her the satisfaction of having me arrested again. The last time I did that it took forever for that story to die down and besides, the creators of my show told me that another arrest would surely get me fired and Wu-Wu Tanner would be no more.

That was not an option.

So, I held my back straight, proceeded to the shower, snorted two crushed Black Beauties, and once I made my way to Heaven and felt like a star, I dressed in a leopard cat suit, hot pink feather belt tied around my waist, chandelier earrings that rested on my shoulders, five-inch leopard wedged heels, and a chinchilla boa tossed loosely around my neck. I walked over to my full-length mirror and posed. "Mirror, mirror on the wall, who's the boomboom-flyest of 'em all?" I did a Beyoncé booty bounce, swept the floor, and sprang back up.

The mirror didn't respond, but I knew for sure that if it had, it would've said, "You doin' it, Wu-Wu. You boombop-bustin'-it fly!"